Ferris

Ferris

KATE DiCAMILLO

WALKER
BOOKS

First published 2024 by Walker Books Ltd
87 Vauxhall Walk, London SE11 5HJ

2 4 6 8 10 9 7 5 3 1

Text © 2024 Kate DiCamillo
Jacket and interior illustrations © 2024 David Litchfield

This book has been typeset in Dante MT Pro

Printed and bound by CPI Group (UK) Ltd, Croydon CR0 4YY

British Library Cataloguing in Publication Data:
a catalogue record for this book is available from the British Library

ISBN 978-1-5295-1912-9

www.walker.co.uk

MIX
Paper | Supporting
responsible forestry
FSC® C171272

For Rainey Stewart and Tracey Bailey

1

It was the summer before Emma Phineas Wilkey (whom everyone called Ferris) went into the fifth grade.

It was the summer that the ghost appeared to Charisse, the summer that Ferris's sister, Pinky Wilkey, devoted herself to becoming an outlaw, and the summer that Uncle Ted left Aunt Shirley and moved into the Wilkey basement to paint a history of the world.

It was the summer that Ferris's best friend, Billy Jackson, played a song called "Mysterious Barricades" over and over again on the piano.

Billy Jackson loved music.

The very first sentence he had ever spoken to Ferris was, "I hear piano music in my head all the time, and, I wonder, would it be all right if I held on to your hand?"

They were standing in Mrs Bleeker's kindergarten classroom. Squares of sunlight were shining on the wooden floors, and Ferris gave her hand to Billy Jackson while he continued to explain to her about the piano music in his head.

Billy's hand was sweating. His glasses were attached to his head with a strap, and Ferris knew almost immediately, from that very first moment, that she didn't want to ever lose hold of Billy Jackson. She said, "There's a piano at our house. You can come over and play it whenever you want."

It was a big, old house, the house where Ferris lived.

Ferris had her own bedroom. So did Pinky, and so did Ferris's parents.

Charisse, Ferris's grandmother, had her own room too.

That was where the ghost showed up – on the threshold of Charisse's room.

"Darling," Charisse said to Ferris, "this ghost!

She just stands there in the doorway and stares at me with the most mournful expression."

"What does she look like?" said Ferris. "Besides mournful?"

"She's wearing a long dress. She has a handkerchief in her hand, and she wrings and squeezes it. Clearly, she is in despair over something. She is very unhappy, darling."

"Are there happy ghosts?" said Ferris.

"I would like you to know that Boomer sees her too. In case you are inclined to doubt my sanity."

Boomer was the dog. He was part sheepdog and part German Shepherd, and also, according to Ferris's father, part woolly mammoth. No one was sure, really, *what* kind of dog Boomer was, only that he was enormous and furry.

"Boomer refuses to enter the room if he sees her standing there," said Charisse. "He is a very perceptive dog."

"But why is the ghost here?" asked Ferris. She was sitting in the window seat of Charisse's room, looking out into the backyard.

Ferris figured that she had spent more than half her time on earth in Charisse's room – talking to her grandmother, listening to her, playing gin rummy with her and reading to her from the Bible and also from a battered paperback copy of Walt Whitman's *Leaves of Grass*.

"I mean," said Ferris, "what do you think the ghost wants?"

"I have absolutely no idea," said Charisse. "I am utterly baffled by all of it, darling."

Boomer was asleep on the rose-patterned carpet by Charisse's bed. He was moving his paws, breathing heavily, dreaming of chasing something. The one time Boomer had actually managed to catch something (a baby squirrel), he had dropped it immediately and crept into the house with his tail between his legs – devastated by shame and regret.

His was a gentle soul.

That was what Charisse said about Boomer. "His is a gentle soul."

"Are you afraid of her?" said Ferris. "Are you afraid of the ghost?"

"When you've lived as long as I have," said Charisse, who was seventy-three years old, "you are not afraid of ghosts."

"What *are* you afraid of, then?" said Ferris.

"Indignities," said Charisse.

"I don't understand," said Ferris.

"Isn't that wonderful?" said Charisse. "I'm so pleased that you don't understand."

It was late afternoon, and Charisse was in bed.

"Why are you still in bed?" asked Ferris.

"I don't feel well, darling, and that is all I want to say about that. I would ask you not to question me to death, as is your wont."

Ferris was Charisse's favourite person on the planet. No one denied it – not Charisse, not Ferris, not anybody in the whole household.

Charisse was the person who had caught Ferris when she entered the world – literally caught her.

Charisse had been on her knees in the dirt of the fairground, and she had been the one who had seen Ferris first. She said she recognized her at first sight.

"Welcome, darling." That is what she had said

to Ferris, and Ferris swore that she could remember it – entering the world, seeing the blue sky, seeing Charisse's face smiling down at her.

"It's a love story," Charisse said whenever she told the story of Ferris being born. "But then every story is a love story. Or every *good* story is a love story."

"You can't possibly remember it," said Ferris's mother that evening. "*I* barely remember it. You know what your grandmother does? She dramatizes everything. No, she romanticizes everything. Going into labour on a patch of dirt at the fairground is not romantic, I can tell you that much. Hand me the sponge, will you?"

Ferris and her mother were at the kitchen table. Her mother was pasting Green Stamps into an S&H Green Stamps book. She was working on filling enough books to get a sandwich toaster.

Ferris's mother was practical. She was a pragmatist. She taught high school maths. "Attempting to teach maths to a roomful of teenagers on a daily basis leaves no room for romantic notions," her mother often said. "I am a pragmatist through and through."

Was Ferris a pragmatist or a romantic?

She didn't know.

But sometimes, right before she fell asleep, she saw blue sky – the blue sky that she remembered from being born – and she saw Charisse smiling at her, her face lit up and beautiful.

Ferris believed that she'd recognized Charisse as soon as she had laid eyes on her.

Just the same way she'd recognized Billy Jackson from the first day she took his hand.

"Every story is a love story," Ferris said out loud to herself that night when she was in bed.

The windows in her room were open. The crickets were singing. Boomer had thrown himself across her feet. He was snoring.

It was hot having a woolly mammoth draped across her feet, but Ferris was worried about Charisse not feeling well, and she was worried about the ghost – what did she want? Why was she only appearing to Charisse? And so Ferris was grateful to have Boomer there, anchoring her to the bed, the house, the world.

"I am ten years old," Ferris said into the darkness.

Ten seemed like a significant number of years.

Ten seemed like the age when Ferris might start to understand some things.

"I am ten years old, and every story is a love story."

Above her, above the house, the stars were shining, wheeling their way across the sky.

Boomer snored.

The crickets sang.

It sounded like maybe the stars were singing too.

Ferris closed her eyes. She listened.

Every story is a love story, the whole world seemed to be singing. *Every good story is a love story.*

2

Ferris's aunt Shirley was a cosmetologist.

"I am not a beautician. I am not a barber. I do not simply *cut* hair," Aunt Shirley said to anybody who expressed an interest in her vocation (and also to those who did not).

"What I am is a cosmetologist," Shirley said. "I have a cosmetology *degree*. I am a businesswoman."

Aunt Shirley owned a beauty salon called Shirley Curl.

The letter *y* in the Shirley Curl sign came up underneath the word *Curl* and formed a sprightly curlicue. Under "Shirley Curl" it read: "Why Not Look Your Best!"

Ferris thought "Why Not Look Your Best" should have a question mark after it, but Shirley did not want a question mark. She wanted an exclamation mark.

"I am not interested in sowing doubt," Aunt Shirley said to Uncle Ted when he made the sign for her. "It is every woman's right to be beautiful. Do *not* put a question mark on my sign. You must be emphatic."

Uncle Ted had a PhD in philosophy, and he had worked as a professional sign painter until the news was suddenly delivered to him that he must paint a visual history of the world.

"Who delivered that news to him exactly?" asked Ferris's mother.

"I'm not certain," said Ferris's father. "But I do believe someone delivered something to him." Ted was his younger brother, and her father understood him on what he often referred to as a "cellular level".

"Delusions of grandeur," said Ferris's mother. "He's a romantic. Just like Charisse."

"Now honey," said Ferris's father, "let's just see where the dust settles here."

"The dust has already settled," said her mother.

"Ted's living in the basement, isn't he?"

They were in the kitchen, sitting at the yellow table. Ferris's father was reading the paper. Ferris's mother was pasting more Green Stamps into the Green Stamps book. Actually, she was *pounding* Green Stamps.

Boomer was under the table. He thumped his tail approvingly every time Ferris's mother pounded another stamp into place. Outside the kitchen window the magnolia tree was standing solemnly, patiently, its glossy green leaves reflecting the morning light.

It was the first day of the summer holidays.

Ferris had her bare feet on Boomer's hairy flank. She was drinking coffee with a lot of cream and sugar in it. Her father had handed her the cup and said, "I think a ten-year-old can join her parents in a morning cup of coffee."

Pinky was running around the garden. She had on a black cape, and she was shouting the same sentence over and over, louder each time: "Out of my way, fools!"

Pinky was six years old, and even though Ferris was her older sister, she did not understand Pinky on a cellular level.

Pinky was a fearsome mystery.

Charisse was in her room, sleeping (which was worrisome) and Uncle Ted was in the basement.

"The dust," said Ferris's mother, "has settled into a blanket of certainty. We'll never get Ted out of that basement."

"It's his house too," said Ferris's father. He rattled the paper. "It's his ancestral home as well as mine."

Ferris's mother snorted. She said, "Ancestral home." She snorted again. "I bet Shirley is relieved to be rid of him."

Ferris took a sip of coffee. It was rich, mysterious. It tasted like being an adult.

"I do not want him living in the basement indefinitely," said Ferris's mother. "I am not raising another child."

"Honey," said Ferris's father. "I'm sure he's not expecting you to raise him. Also, he can hear you."

"Good," said her mother. She pounded a foot on the kitchen floor at the same time as she pounded another Green Stamp into place.

Boomer sat up and barked.

From outside came the sound of Pinky shouting (again), "Out of my way, fools!"

Ferris took another sip of coffee. She said, "Charisse doesn't feel well."

"She's old," said Ferris's mother. Which didn't seem like a very reassuring thing to say. Her mother often fell short in the reassurance department.

Ferris said, "I think I'll go and see Uncle Ted." She put down her cup of coffee and got up and went to the pantry and retrieved the big jar of peanuts. Uncle Ted loved peanuts.

Boomer came out from underneath the kitchen table and followed her. He loved peanuts too.

"Do not leave that jar down there with Ted," said her mother.

"OK," said Ferris.

The stairs down to the basement were creaky and dark and cobwebbed. Ferris and Boomer descended slowly. Ferris held the jar of peanuts out in front of her. She felt as if she was carrying a lantern.

"Ferris!" said Ted when he saw her.

"Hi, Uncle Ted," said Ferris. "I brought you some peanuts."

"You are a deeply thoughtful child, honey," said Ted.

"OK," said Ferris. She handed Ted the jar. "How's the history of the world going?"

"Would you like to see?" said Ted.

Ferris nodded. Ted escorted her over behind the boiler, where there was a gigantic white canvas with a small lump in the left-hand corner. Ferris stepped closer. She peered at the lump. It looked like maybe it could be a foot.

"Is that a foot?" she said.

"Yes," said Ted.

Ferris said, "It looks good."

She wasn't sure exactly what a foot had to do with the history of the world.

"I had to start somewhere," said Uncle Ted. "A foot seemed like a good place."

Ferris nodded again. Ted unscrewed the lid to the peanut jar, tipped the jar back and poured peanuts directly into his mouth.

He was still in his bathrobe. His hair was sticking out on either side of his head and also on the top.

Ferris went back to studying the foot. It seemed like the polite thing to do.

"Ferris, honey, I have a favour to ask you," said Uncle Ted.

"OK," said Ferris.

"I wonder if you could go down to Shirley Curl and find out what Shirley is thinking."

"Thinking about what?"

"About me, honey. See if she misses me. I'm asking you to spy. I'm asking you to be a spy in the house of love."

Uncle Ted tipped the peanut jar and poured more peanuts into his mouth.

Boomer barked. Ted looked down at him.

"He wants a peanut," said Ferris.

Ted tossed Boomer a peanut.

"Wouldn't Pinky be a better spy?" said Ferris.

"Your little sister is a proper terror. Yes, she is. A genuine terror. That child would be entirely at home with Robespierre. However, she lacks subtlety. You do not."

"Who's Robespierre?" said Ferris.

"He was a French revolutionary, honey," said Ted. He turned back to the canvas and stared at the foot.

The basement smelt like cobwebs and bathrobe and oil paints. And peanuts.

Why, Ferris wondered, would you start painting the history of the world with a single foot? And how could you ever hope to paint something as complicated as the world and its history anyway?

Ferris licked her lips. She tasted coffee, adulthood.

"OK," she said. "I'll try to be a spy."

3

Aunt Shirley was blonde and pink. She looked like someone who had been spun out of sugar and placed on top of an elaborate celebratory cake.

"Now, Ferris, you have some beautiful hair, but you don't tend to it right," said Aunt Shirley. "You do not *own* your beauty."

Ferris had gone to Shirley Curl to spy on Aunt Shirley, and somehow she had ended up sitting in the beauty chair with a flowered gown tied around her neck.

"I believe I'll set it," said Shirley in a meditative voice.

"Set what?" said Ferris.

Shirley swatted at Ferris's shoulder. "Hush up, now," she said. "I'm going to make you just as pretty as God intended you to be." She turned away and started mixing up chemicals in a bowl.

Outside the shop was the sunlit street, which from the vantage point of the beauty chair seemed absolutely paradisical to Ferris.

Boomer was standing in front of the plate-glass door, staring in at her. Shirley didn't believe in dogs in beauty salons. "It sends entirely the wrong message," she'd said. "Particularly with that dog. Who is unkempt in the extreme."

Ferris waved at Boomer. He pricked his ears and wagged his tail in return.

"'Tell the truth, Emma Phineas!" Shirley suddenly shouted. She twirled round and pointed at Ferris with a hair-encrusted brush. "Ted sent you here to spy on me, didn't he?"

"Yes, ma'am, he did!" Ferris shouted back.

"I knew it," said Shirley. "I just knew it. Let me tell you something." She pointed the brush at Ferris again. "Charisse has done that son of hers no favours. You cannot tell someone that they are a genius from the minute they arrive in the world without them starting to believe you. And then what happens?"

"I don't know," said Ferris.

"I'll tell you what happens," said Shirley. "They *believe* that they are a genius, and they quit their job and they get the ludicrous..." Shirley stopped talking for a second or two. She said the word *ludicrous* again, slowly – savouring it, like she couldn't believe what a perfect word it was.

Ludicrous meant foolish, unreasonable.

Ferris knew this because Mrs Mielk, her fourth-grade teacher, had been vocabulary-obsessed.

"Vocabulary is the key to the kingdom!" said Mrs Mielk. "All of life hinges on knowing the right word to use at the right time."

The difference, Mrs Mielk said, between the right word and the almost-right word was the difference between lightning and the lightning bug.

"Mr Mark Twain said that," said Mrs Mielk. "That is a quote from Mr Mark Twain, wordsmith extraordinaire."

Mrs Mielk had crooked teeth. She was impatient.

She stamped her left foot (never her right foot, only her left foot) when she got angry, and she got angry often. She was not an altogether likable person, but Ferris loved her because Mrs Mielk had given Ferris and Billy Jackson the gift of words.

Together, Ferris and Billy had worked to memorize definitions and spellings for test after test. And in the process, the words had lodged themselves permanently in Ferris's brain and heart. They were hers.

"The truly *ludicrous*," continued Shirley, saying the word for the third time, "notion that God has picked you to paint the history of the world. And not to hold down a job while you are painting this *history* of the world? That is *ludicrous*."

"Yes, ma'am," said Ferris. As if she agreed. Which she kind of did.

Shirley started to put curlers in Ferris's hair, and Ferris wished that someone would come and rescue her.

The door to Shirley Curl opened, and Twilla Dormin walked in.

Twilla Dormin would not rescue anyone from anything, ever. Twilla was mean. She had taught Sunday school for years. She made kids cry by describing in great detail what it would be like to burn in Hell for all eternity.

"Howdy, howdy," said Twilla in her deceptively singsong voice.

"Hey, Miss Twilla," said Shirley and Ferris in unison.

"I'll be right with you," said Shirley.

"That's fine," said Twilla. "That's just fine. Now, is that Ferris Wilkey I see? Is that Ferris sitting there and getting her hair done like a proper young lady?"

"Yes, ma'am," said Ferris. "It's me."

"About time," said Miss Twilla. "About time you grew up and acted like a lady instead of running around all over the place with that strange little Billy Jackson. Shirley, is it true that Ted moved out? I am so sorry for you and all of your suffering."

"Go on and get yourself a magazine and sit down, Twilla," said Shirley in a very firm voice. "I will be right with you."

Shirley waited until Twilla had sat down and picked up a copy of *Good Housekeeping* that had a picture of a jelly mould on the cover.

"And now it has all come to fruition," whispered Shirley into Ferris's ear. "All that praise has done him in. Now he believes himself to be the next Mona Lisa."

"*Mona Lisa* is a painting," said Ferris.

"I know that!" shouted Shirley. And then she went back to whispering. "Tell me, honey, have you seen the painting? How does it look?"

Which is how Ferris, without intending to, ended up describing the foot blob to Shirley.

"A *foot*?" shrieked Shirley as she slathered Ferris's hair in permanent solution. "What do you mean, a foot?"

"It's a really good foot," said Ferris. Even though she didn't think it was much of a foot.

"What is it you two are talking about?" said Twilla.

"Nothing, Miss Twilla," said Shirley and Ferris together.

The permanent smell was making Ferris dizzy.

She couldn't believe how quickly things had spun out of control.

"I feel funny," Ferris said to Shirley.

"Well, I feel funny too," said Shirley. "But not in a laughing way. Not in a ha-ha kind of way."

"I don't see where anything at all is funny," said Twilla.

Which she didn't need to say.

Nobody had ever heard Twilla Dormin laugh.

4

There was a lot of laughter at the dinner table that night.

Most of it came from Pinky.

"You look like you stuck your finger in an electric socket," said Pinky to Ferris. "You do not look like a proper outlaw."

Why, Ferris wondered, did Pinky have to be so objectionable at every possible juncture?

"I know I don't look like a proper outlaw," said Ferris. "I don't want to be a proper outlaw."

Pinky stopped laughing. "Well then," she said, "something is wrong with you."

"No," said Ferris. "Something's wrong with *you*."

"That's enough," said Ferris's mother.

"You look like Shirley Temple, honey," said Ferris's father. "I mean, if you squint a little, that's how you look."

"I don't understand how it happened," said her mother.

"Aunt Shirley did it," said Ferris.

"Yes," said her mother. "But why?"

They were in the dining room, sitting beneath the old chandelier – which was not lit because it had never been wired for electricity.

Ferris looked over at Charisse. Charisse put her hand on top of Ferris's hand. They were sitting beside each other. They always sat beside each other.

"I'm going to get my name on a Wanted poster," said Pinky. "That's my plan."

"That's not really a plan, honey," said Ferris's father. "That's more like what you would call a pipe dream."

Pinky slammed her butter knife on the table. Everyone jumped.

"It's a plan," Pinky said. And then she muttered under her breath, "Out of my way, fools."

"Mother, how are you feeling?" said Ferris's father to Charisse.

"Unwell," said Charisse. "Will Theodore be joining us for dinner?"

"I'm not hosting a dinner party, Charisse," said Ferris's mother. "If Ted wants to get out of his bathrobe and come up the stairs and sit down at the table and eat with us, he is perfectly welcome to do that. But did I extend him a gilded invitation? No, I did not."

"What does 'gilded' mean?" said Pinky.

"Golden," said Ferris, glad to be able to sound like an older sister and tell Pinky something she didn't know.

Gilded had been a Mielk vocabulary word.

"Outlaws are extremely interested in gold," said Pinky.

Monomaniacal. That was another Mielk vocabulary word. It described Pinky perfectly. She was only interested in one thing: being an outlaw.

Boomer moved around the table, going from person to person, putting his head on knees and thighs, wagging his tail hopefully.

Ferris watched Pinky toss him an entire buttered roll. Boomer swallowed it without chewing and gave Pinky a look full of love and gratitude.

"Come here, Boomer," said Ferris. He came over and sat down next to her.

"In other news," said Ferris's father, "it seems that we have a raccoon in the attic. A dancing raccoon. At least that is what it sounds like. No need to worry, though! This is just a general public service announcement."

"A raccoon dancing in the attic and Ted in the basement painting a history of the world," said Ferris's mother. "That just about sums it all up." She sighed.

"Theodore has it in him to do something great," said Charisse. Her voice shook with indignation.

"We all have it in us to do something great," said Ferris's mother. "Most of us don't do it."

"I'm going to be an outlaw!" shouted Pinky. "And that's great!"

"There's nothing great about being a criminal," said Ferris.

"Everyone should just calm down," said Ferris's father. He was always suggesting that people calm down. He was a very mild-mannered man. That was how he described himself. "I am nothing but a mild-mannered man who loves the world and all its creatures," he said often.

Ferris pulled her hand out from underneath Charisse's trembling hand. She put hers on top. And then Charisse pulled her hand out from the bottom and put it on top of Ferris's. It was something they had done for as long as Ferris could remember. One or other of their hands was always on top, protecting, and the other hand was underneath, protected.

Every story is a love story.

From the living room came the sound of piano playing.

That meant Billy Jackson had arrived.

Ferris's heart lifted up.

"That song," said Ferris's mother.

"It's beautiful," said Charisse.

"It's called 'Mysterious Barricades'," said Ferris.

"It's really old." She moved her hand out from underneath Charisse's hand and put it on top, protecting.

"Billy!" shouted Ferris's mother. "Come on in here and eat with us. We saved you a place."

There was always a place for Billy Jackson at the Wilkey table. Ferris's mother loved him. They all loved him.

"Yes, ma'am," Billy Jackson called back. "In a minute."

Boomer put his head on Ferris's thigh, and Ferris held still and listened as Billy Jackson played his mysterious song.

Ferris's mother said, "Charisse, you said you are unwell."

"I am," said Charisse.

"Should we make an appointment with Dr Trench?" said Ferris's mother.

"I suppose," said Charisse.

Ferris felt something cold and shivery run through her.

She squeezed her grandmother's hand.

The piano music stopped, and Billy Jackson came into the dining room.

"Hey," he said, standing in the doorway.

"Hey," said Ferris.

"Your hair got all fuzzy," said Billy Jackson in a voice of wonder.

Pinky laughed loudly. "Fuzzy Ferris," she said, and then her face turned thoughtful. "I think I'm going to rob a bank," she said. "That's probably the quickest way to become an outlaw."

It turned out that Pinky was serious.

It turned out to be a serious time in general, in Ferris's world.

5

When Ferris was a baby, her father referred to her as "that child who had the audacity to make her entrance beneath the Ferris wheel".

"You are my sweet Ferris-wheel baby," he said again and again. And then he shortened it to "Sweet Ferris", and then he shortened it again and just called her "Ferris", and it stuck.

No one used her real name very much except for Charisse, who sometimes called her *Emmaphineas* – pushing the two names together and making them into one long word, a word that sounded like it could appear on a Mielk vocabulary list, a word that Ferris could spell but couldn't define. Was Emmaphineas an exotic flower? A famous ship? Some strange malady?

"Emmaphineas," said Charisse very quietly.

They were together in Charisse's room. Charisse was in bed and Ferris was on the window seat. Billy Jackson was waiting downstairs.

"Do you want to play cards?" said Ferris.

"I do not," said Charisse. "Go on with Billy Jackson. I am just fine, darling."

The fan in the window was spinning in a lazy, half-hearted way, and the room smelled like the Florida water (cloves and cinnamon and sweet orange) that Charisse dabbed on her wrists and neck every morning and night.

Ferris's scalp itched. She kept seeing pieces of her strange, frizzy hair out of the corner of her eye. It alarmed her. It was like having a wild animal crouching on top of her head.

"Shirley has done you no favours with that perm," said Charisse.

"I know it," said Ferris. She sighed.

"It will be fine, darling," said Charisse.

"What will be?" said Ferris.

"Everything," said Charisse.

"I was thinking," said Ferris. "What if the ghost

is here because you don't feel well?"

"Do you mean to imply that the ghost has come to collect me for the next world? That she is here to escort me to the Great Beyond?" Charisse laughed. "Well, I wouldn't mind leaving."

"Don't say that," said Ferris.

"We come and go, darling. That's what we do. Speaking of which: your dog is waiting for you. And your friend. Go on, now."

Boomer was sitting in the doorway, staring at Ferris and panting. There were breadcrumbs in his whiskers.

"I'll be right there," Ferris said to him, and then she looked over at Charisse and saw that she was asleep with her hands crossed over her stomach and a smile on her lips.

Ferris had a sudden intimation of things to come, of the world, Ferris's world, without Charisse in it.

Intimation was a Mielk vocabulary word.

It meant an indication. A hint.

Ferris got up off the window seat and went and shook Charisse by the shoulder.

Charisse opened her eyes. She looked at Ferris like she had no idea who she was.

"It's me," said Ferris.

"Darling," said Charisse. She blinked. "I know. I would recognize you anywhere. Even with that ridiculous hairdo. Go run with Billy Jackson. You wouldn't believe how much of your life you spend not getting to run."

"OK," said Ferris. "But I'll be back."

"Of course you will," said Charisse. She closed her eyes.

When Ferris walked out of Charisse's room, she felt something strange brush up against her, as if she was stepping through a silvery curtain.

"I think I felt it," said Ferris, turning back to Charisse. "I felt the ghost."

Her grandmother's eyes were closed. She said nothing in response.

From downstairs, Billy Jackson called, "Come on, Ferris. Let's go!"

And she went.

6

Ferris and Billy Jackson ran. They ran with Boomer running alongside them and running ahead of them, stopping to sniff things and then running again, working to catch them up.

Ferris's hair felt funny, but the rest of her felt good. Her legs were strong. And so was her heart. She thought that maybe she could run for ever and ever.

She and Billy Jackson and Boomer ran downtown, past Shirley Curl and Buoy Hardware and the Furnace Dime store and Ferris's father's office (Wilkey and Sons, Architects).

They ran to Big Billy Jackson's Steakhouse.

Big Billy Jackson was Billy Jackson's father. He had been a famous American-football player, and now he owned the steakhouse. Uncle Ted had painted the sign in front of the restaurant. It was a giant portrait of Big Billy Jackson holding a ball in one hand and a steak in the other, and there were words coming out of Big Billy's mouth in a cartoon bubble that said, "I am Big Billy Jackson and I know how to do two things: Throw a Ball and Cook a Steak."

People came to the restaurant so they could get their picture taken with Big Billy.

They said, "Big Billy, I have always been such a fan." And "Big Billy, nobody in the history of the world played ball like you." And "Big Billy, I hear you have a son. Is he working to carry on the football tradition?"

"My son," Big Billy would say, "is a piano player. He plays classical music. And he comes in here every day and practises on the steakhouse piano. Ain't that something? You never do have to ask him to practise. Every day, he plays his music and it is beautiful."

Big Billy smiled so big and proud when he talked about Billy Jackson that no one ever said, "What in the world, Big Billy? How could you let a boy of yours mess around with a piano? Why aren't you putting a ball in that child's hands? Why?"

"Look at my hands!" Big Billy would say. "Look at these old mitts!" Big Billy Jackson's hands looked like hams. "I couldn't never play the piano. Never in a million years. And my boy was born to play the piano! Been hearing piano music in his head since he got here. Been playing the piano since before he could even talk. Ain't it something? Ain't it the biggest mystery you ever heard of?"

No one argued with him. They all agreed it was a mystery.

So many things were mysteries. That was what Ferris thought as she sat on the roof of Big Billy Jackson's Steakhouse.

The air above the restaurant smelt like steak and mashed potatoes and hot tar. The roof was flat and warm from the sun beating down on it all day.

Ferris and Billy Jackson sat side by side.

Billy was humming, looking up at the sky. The last of the evening light glinted off his glasses.

"I think Charisse needs to go to the doctor," said Ferris.

Billy Jackson lowered his head. He turned to Ferris. "What's wrong with her?"

Ferris shrugged. Out of the corner of her eye she saw one of her frizzy curls bounce up and down. The word *ignoble* went through her head, and she said it out loud. "Ignoble."

Ignoble was a Mielk vocabulary word.

Billy Jackson spelt it and then Ferris defined it, because that was the way they had studied together for all of fourth grade – taking turns spelling and defining, defining and spelling.

"I-G-N-O-B-L-E," said Billy Jackson.

"Not honourable," said Ferris.

And then she knew why the word had popped into her head. She was feeling ignoble about having described Uncle Ted's painting to Aunt Shirley.

She told Billy Jackson how she had been sent to spy on Aunt Shirley and how she had ended up betraying Ted by talking about the foot.

"He's just painted the one foot?" said Billy Jackson.

"Yes," said Ferris.

"History has a lot of feet in it," said Billy. He was quiet for a minute. "I guess you got to start somewhere."

"Yeah, that's what Uncle Ted said. I just wish I hadn't told Shirley about it." Ferris was glad Ted hadn't shown up for dinner. She didn't want to explain to him how she had failed. "Also," said Ferris, "there are other problems. My dad says there's a raccoon in the attic. And Charisse is seeing a ghost."

"A real ghost?" said Billy Jackson.

"I think so. Charisse says that Boomer sees her too. It's a woman ghost, wearing a long dress and carrying a handkerchief."

Boomer barked. He was barking for Ferris and Billy Jackson to come down, and he was also barking because sometimes if he barked loud enough and long enough, Pearl – the head cook at Big Billy Jackson's Steakhouse – would come banging out the kitchen door and give him a bone.

Billy Jackson smiled. "Boomer is down there hoping for a bone."

"The dogs bark but the caravan passes by," said Ferris.

The dogs bark but the caravan passes by was something that Ferris's father said all the time. He said it just as often as he said he was a mild-mannered man who loved the world and all its creatures.

"What does that mean, though, about the caravan and the dogs?" said Billy.

"I guess it means you can bark about what you want, or shout about it, but that the world doesn't care that much really; it just keeps on doing what it's doing."

"What I want is to travel all over the world and play the piano," said Billy Jackson. "What do you want?"

"I want Charisse to live for ever," said Ferris.

Billy Jackson took hold of Ferris's hand. She could feel the music in him. His fingers thrummed and buzzed the way guitar strings did after you plucked them.

"Charisse says that every story is a love story," said Ferris.

"Yeah," said Billy. "I know."

"Do you believe it, though?"

Billy Jackson looked up at the sky. "Yes," he said.

Boomer barked again. The screen door to the steakhouse creaked open.

"You big old mess of a dog," Ferris heard Pearl say. "You big mess. I ain't never in my life seen a dog with so much fur. I can't tell one end of you from the other."

The screen door banged shut.

Ferris leant forward and looked over the edge of the roof. Boomer was standing with a big bone in his mouth, wagging his tail.

"But what's the point of love if people die?" Ferris said, still staring down at Boomer.

"That's what music is for," said Billy Jackson.

Which wasn't really an answer; but still, it seemed like one.

Billy Jackson started to hum.

"'Mysterious Barricades'," said Ferris.

Billy Jackson nodded. He kept humming.

The two of them sat on the roof of the steakhouse

until the first pinpricks of stars appeared, and then they walked back to Ferris's house, Boomer trotting behind them carrying his big steak bone, Billy Jackson still humming, bats flitting around their heads, the crickets singing and singing – music everywhere.

7

On Monday, Ferris and her mother and Charisse and Pinky went to the Devon Medical Center to see what was wrong with Charisse.

Charisse wore a flowery dress. Pinky had on her black cape, and Ferris's permed hair seemed to have grown even fuzzier and wilder.

"It's a permanent," said her mother. "That's what it's called. A *permanent*. That means you're in it for the long haul. Think about that the next time you stop in to visit your aunt Shirley."

Ferris thought about it. It didn't cheer her up much.

"Hello hello," said Dr Trench when he came into the examining room and found the four of them waiting for him. "How exciting! It's the travelling circus."

"Something like that," said Ferris's mother. She sighed.

"How are you, Sarah?" said Dr Trench.

"I'm fine. It's Charisse we're worried about."

"Hop up on the examining table, Mrs Wilkey," said Dr Trench. "We'll take a look under the hood."

"Hop up on the table?" said Charisse, her voice dripping with disdain.

Dr Trench smiled. "Now now, Mrs Wilkey," he said.

"Hop up on the table and you'll *look under the hood*?" said Charisse.

"Let me try again," said Dr Trench. "If you would be so kind as to climb up on the examining table, Mrs Wilkey."

Charisse stood up. With her head held high and her handbag held close, she stepped towards the table.

"Do you want help?" said Ferris.

"I do not, darling," said Charisse. She smiled at her. "It is, however, very kind of you to offer."

"I danced with your father, you know," Charisse said to Dr Trench once she was up on the table.

Ferris thought Dr Trench seemed too old to have a father. His face was lined and weary-looking.

"Oakley Trench. He and I danced together at the VFW," said Charisse. "He was not a good dancer, but it made no difference. We were young."

"I see," said Dr Trench. "Please stick out your tongue, Mrs Wilkey."

"I'm not here about my tongue."

"I can show you my tongue," said Pinky. She was standing next to Dr Trench, her black cape trailing on the floor.

"No need," said Dr Trench to Pinky without turning around. "What are you here about then, Mrs Wilkey?"

"I have puffy feet," said Charisse. "And swollen ankles. I've never had puffy feet or swollen ankles. It's unsightly. I've always prided myself on my elegant feet and my shapely ankles."

"Tell him how you *feel*, Charisse," said Ferris's mother. "Not how you look. How you feel."

"Will you pull out my loose tooth?" said Pinky to Dr Trench.

Dr Trench looked down at Pinky and studied her for a minute. "You're a tough customer. I bet you could do it yourself with a pair of pliers." He winked.

"Sit down, Pinky," said Ferris's mother.

"No," said Pinky, and she left the examining room with an angry swirl of her black cape.

Ferris was relieved to see her go.

"Come back here," said Ferris's mother. But she didn't say it like she meant it.

Dr Trench put his stethoscope on Charisse's chest and listened intently. He looked like someone trying to crack a safe, working to get the combination to Charisse.

"Hmmm," said Dr Trench.

Ferris felt a sense of foreboding.

She spelled the Mielk vocabulary word quietly to herself.

F-O-R-E-B-O-D-I-N-G.

She imagined Billy Jackson standing beside her, defining the word.

"A feeling that something bad is going to happen," she heard Billy Jackson say.

"Hmmm," said Dr Trench again, the stethoscope still on Charisse's chest.

"Hmmm," repeated Charisse. She rolled her eyes and stuck out her tongue at Ferris, and Ferris was suddenly overcome by love for her grandmother – for her elegant feet and shapely ankles, her gnarled hands and bright eyes, her refusal to follow directions, her insistence on not letting anybody tell her who to be.

"You are too much of a rule follower, Ferris," Charisse had said to her once. "You have to insist on being yourself. Do not let the world tell you who you are. Rather, tell the world who you are. Pinky understands this. She takes it to an extreme, of course."

Ferris made sure that Dr Trench couldn't see her, and then she stuck her tongue out at Charisse.

Charisse laughed, and Ferris felt another wave of love roll over her. The wave was so strong, so bright, that she had to bend over and take a deep breath.

"What in the world are you doing, Ferris?" said

her mother, who was digging through her handbag looking for something.

There came a scream from somewhere in the building.

"Oh no," said Ferris's mother, looking up from her bag. "Pinky."

"Pinky," said Ferris.

"Go and get her," said her mother.

"Why do I always have to go and get her?" said Ferris.

"You're her sister, that's why. Go."

8

Ferris stepped out of the examining room and bumped into a nurse whose name tag read MARLA DEAN.

"Excuse me," said Ferris.

Marla Dean was staring down at the palm of her left hand in wonder. There was some blood. Actually, there was quite a lot of blood.

"She bit me," said Marla Dean, still looking at her hand. "She was wearing a black cape, and she had the most beautiful face. She had the face of an angel, and she bit me."

Pinky *did* have the face of an angel – evidence, said Ferris's father, of the universe having a fantastic and highly developed sense of humour.

"'Where are you going in such a hurry,

sweetheart?' That's what I said to her," said Marla Dean. "And I put out my hand, just … you know? As a calming gesture? And she took hold of it and bit me! She bit my hand."

"I'm sorry," said Ferris. It occurred to her that she would probably spend the rest of her life apologizing for Pinky. She started to run down the hallway.

She looked in all the examining rooms, and then she went out to the waiting room, where she found Pinky sitting in an orange plastic chair with her legs crossed, turning the pages of a *Highlights* magazine.

"Your hair looks stupid," said Pinky when she saw Ferris. "I can't believe how stupid it looks." She bent her head and went back to studying the magazine. She turned a page. She had a very peaceful look on her face.

"Did you bite a nurse named Marla Dean?" said Ferris.

"I am an outlaw wanted in all fifty states!" shouted Pinky. She threw the magazine down and went racing out of the automatic doors of the clinic, her cape flying behind her.

"Is that your sister?" said the receptionist.

"No," said Ferris.

"You have such interesting hair."

"Thank you," said Ferris.

She walked past the receptionist and through the doors and out into the parking lot, where, of course, Pinky was nowhere to be seen.

That was how the visit to the doctor's went.

It wasn't until later in the day that Ferris learntwhat Dr Trench had said – that Charisse's heart wasn't working the way it should.

"How should it work?" said Ferris to her mother.

They were sitting at the kitchen table. The magnolia tree was standing outside the window, looking in at them, listening.

"It's not pumping efficiently," said her mother.

Below them, in the basement, Uncle Ted was painting the history of the world. Ferris's father was in the attic assessing the raccoon situation.

Before he'd climbed the attic stairs, he'd said, "I believe we may have more than one."

"More than one what?" said Ferris's mother.

"Raccoon," said her father.

"Larger problems loom on the horizon," said Ferris's mother.

"The dogs bark but the caravan passes by," said Ferris's father when he left the kitchen and headed for the attic. He took a tennis racket with him for protection.

Pinky was in her room. She had been grounded for an indefinite amount of time as a punishment for biting Marla Dean.

Ferris and her mother had found Pinky downtown in Buoy Hardware, talking to Mr Buoy.

"What a charming child," said Mr Buoy.

Mr Buoy was even older than Charisse. He always wore a bow tie. He had a hearing aid in his left ear.

"It was a delight to converse with her," he said as he fiddled with his hearing aid. "She has a deep interest in all things hardware, particularly pliers."

"Thank you very much, Mr Buoy," Ferris's mother had said as she pushed Pinky ahead of her out of the store.

And now Ferris was sitting across from her mother, and Boomer was resting his head on Ferris's left foot, and Ferris was learning that something was wrong with Charisse.

"What does that mean?" said Ferris. "What does it mean not to pump efficiently?"

Her mother looked her in the eye. She said, "There's water around her heart. And that makes it hard for the heart to work. It's a disease. It's called congestive heart failure."

"Failure?" said Ferris.

"There's medicine for it," her mother said gently. "Dr Trench gave her the medicine."

"OK," said Ferris.

She got up from the table and climbed the stairs to Charisse's room, her heart heavy inside her, Boomer following behind her.

Charisse was asleep in bed, her hands folded on her stomach. Ferris walked into the room, but Boomer sat down in the hallway.

Ferris climbed onto the window seat. She stared hard at the doorway. She wanted desperately to see the ghost but she couldn't see anything except the carpet in the hallway and Boomer's worried face.

She picked up the worn pack of playing cards and shuffled them. Charisse had taught her how to shuffle cards; Charisse had learned from her father. "My father, your great-grandfather, was a rake, darling. A charmer, a ne'er-do-well and a gambler of the worst sort. Why, when I was a child, he gambled this house away. Fortunately, fate intervened. Which is to say that my mother came to the rescue and secured a loan from her father. Those were turbulent times, but then I suppose all times are turbulent in one way or another."

Ferris shuffled the cards again, and then again. They made a fluttery, hopeful sigh. The only other noise in the room was the whistling sound Charisse's breath made as it entered and left her body.

Ferris put down the cards and got up from the window seat. She went to the bed and knelt down and put her left ear on Charisse's chest.

Charisse didn't move.

Ferris listened and she heard it, Charisse's heart.

It was singing a half-broken, half-hopeful song that sounded like *I celebrate myself and sing myself* – Whitman's words from *Leaves of Grass*.

Charisse stirred. She put her hand on top of Ferris's head.

"You strange, wondrous child," she said. "What are you doing?"

"Listening to your heart," said Ferris. She didn't move. "Tell me how you caught me. Tell me how you recognized me at first sight."

"Darling," said Charisse. "She's here."

"Who is?" said Ferris.

"The ghost," said Charisse. "She's standing right in the doorway. Look."

Ferris lifted her head. Boomer was standing to attention. All his fur seemed to be electrified. He made a strange noise – a swallowed, strangled bark.

"I don't see her," said Ferris.

"Shhh," said Charisse.

A great gust of air blew through the room, and the pack of cards went flying up off the window seat. The cards swirled through the air and then landed, scattered all over the floor.

And then there was silence, stillness.

Ferris could hear her own heart beating.

And then she couldn't even hear that.

Everything stopped. The room seemed to hold its breath.

Caesura.

A Mielk vocabulary word – an interruption or break. A silence.

Which was shattered by a high-pitched scream.

"Yeth!" someone shouted. And then, "Out of my way, foolth!"

Pinky.

9

Pinky had pulled out two of her front teeth with a pair of pliers. One tooth had been loose; the other one Pinky had pulled as an "ecthperiment".

There was blood on the floor, little drops that led from Pinky's room down to the kitchen and from there down to the basement, where Pinky had gone to show Uncle Ted her toothless, bloody smile.

"I will not lie," said Uncle Ted. "The child scared me."

They were at the dining room table – Ferris's mother and father, and also Uncle Ted, who was unshaven and wild-eyed and still in his bathrobe, and Billy Jackson, who was sitting next to Ferris, in Charisse's seat.

Charisse had not come down to dinner. She was resting.

Pinky was in her room doing who knows what. Plotting her revenge on someone, most likely.

"The child looked like a ghoul," said Uncle Ted. "She was absolutely dripping blood."

"I'm at my wit's end," said Ferris's mother. "Two teeth! One of them not anywhere near loose."

"They'll grow back," said Ferris's father.

"That's not the point."

"What's the point?"

"The point is, she extracted her own teeth with a pair of pliers! She's six years old! What's going to happen when she's a teenager?"

"Let's not think about that," said Ferris's father.

A door upstairs slammed shut.

"That better not be Pinky," said Ferris's mother. "I told her not to leave her room ever again."

Billy Jackson got up from the table. "Thank you, Mrs Wilkey," he said. "That was a really good supper." He went into the living room and started playing the piano.

"Ferris," said Uncle Ted. "I wonder if I could have a word with you in private."

Ferris's heart sank all the way down to her toes. Now she was going to have to tell Uncle Ted how she had betrayed him, how ignoble she had been.

Plus: Charisse had heart failure! And Pinky had pulled her teeth out with a pair of pliers! And the ghost had thrown a pack of cards!

It was all too much.

"Yes, sir," she said to Uncle Ted.

The sound of "Mysterious Barricades" drifted into the dining room.

"Billy?" called Ferris's mother.

"Yes, ma'am?" Billy Jackson called back, still playing.

"I wonder if there's a different song you could play?" asked Ferris's mother.

The piano music stopped.

Another caesura occurred.

"No, ma'am," said Billy Jackson into the silence. "I mean, this is the song that wants to get played right now."

"I understand," said Ted. "Sometimes you just have to do what the music demands."

"Yes, sir, that's right," said Billy Jackson.

"It's like with me and the painting," said Ted.

Ferris's mother sighed.

Billy Jackson came back into the dining room. "Could I see it?" he said. "Could I see your painting?"

Which is how Ferris and Billy Jackson and Boomer ended up standing with Uncle Ted in the basement, staring at the foot.

"It's harder than I thought it would be. I could see it all in my mind's eye; I truly could. The vision was delivered to me in what I think of as a biblical fashion. I'm not lying, son," Ted said, turning to Billy Jackson. "Angels were moving their wings and sending out waves of light. That's how it felt. But I have to admit that I'm having a hard time living up to that glorious inspiration."

Billy Jackson nodded. He adjusted his glasses. "I understand."

And then Ted turned to Ferris and asked the question she had been dreading. "Did you find out whether Shirley is softening towards me, honey? Do you think she could be working her way towards forgiveness, towards welcoming the prodigal husband home?"

Ferris felt her face get hot. "No," she said. "I mean, I don't know. Because the only thing that happened at the salon was that Shirley permed my hair."

"I did notice that your hairdo was somewhat changed."

Ferris took a big breath and said, "I ended up telling her about the foot, Uncle Ted, and she wasn't very happy, and I'm not sure how any of it really happened."

"The truth of the matter is that no one can outwit Shirley," Uncle Ted said. "She is formidable."

Formidable was a Mielk vocabulary word.

It meant inspiring fear or respect.

"Yes," said Ferris. She touched her hair. "Aunt Shirley is formidable."

Ted sighed. "I suppose the two of you should run along now. Run along before it all becomes too complicated."

Ferris thought that it was too complicated already.

"Charisse has something called congestive heart failure," she said.

Ted nodded. "I heard, honey. I heard. Don't worry. Go on, now. Go out into the world."

He turned away from them and went back to studying the foot. Ferris and Billy Jackson climbed the basement stairs with Boomer following behind them.

Ferris's mother and father were in the kitchen. Her father was washing the dishes and her mother was drying them.

"We're going to the steakhouse," said Ferris.

"That's good," said her father.

The kitchen window was open. The crickets were singing.

"Why do I have the feeling that this is the calm before the storm?" said Ferris's mother. She stared out the window at the magnolia tree.

"The dogs bark…" said Ferris's father.

"Come on," Billy Jackson said to Ferris. "Let's go."

10

It was early afternoon the next day, and yellow light was entering the kitchen and shining on top of the yellow kitchen table – yellow on yellow. Ferris was eating a peanut butter and banana sandwich and trying not to think about Charisse's heart or the ghost. Or Pinky and her teeth. Or betrayal. Boomer was resting his head on her leg, looking up at her with love and hope.

Ferris's mother was reading the paper.

The phone rang. Her mother stood up and answered it.

"Hello," she said. And then, "Yes. This is she." She listened. "Yes," she said again. "Pinky. That's right. Well, Eleanor Rose."

Eleanor Rose was Pinky's real name. No one ever

called her that, of course. Pinky wouldn't allow it. Pinky had been Pinky ever since Ferris had looked at her in the crib and said that the new baby was the same colour as a baby mouse.

"She's all pinky," Ferris had announced.

Ferris had been four years old then and glad to have a sister.

That had been a long time ago.

"I see," said Ferris's mother. "Thank you very much."

She hung up the phone. She looked around the kitchen and then she walked over to the table and picked up a single Green Stamp and licked it and slammed it into the open Green Stamps book. Boomer wagged his tail uncertainly. He looked at Ferris.

"Who was that?" said Ferris.

"The police," said her mother.

"The police?"

"The police. They have your sister."

Ferris's father, home from the office for lunch, wandered into the kitchen and opened the refrigerator and stuck his head inside.

"The police have Pinky?" said Ferris to her mother.

"Heh heh," said Ferris's father. "They should keep her."

Ferris didn't think this was such a bad idea.

Her father's head was still inside the refrigerator. He was holding the *S–SN* volume of the encyclopedia in one hand, using his index finger to mark his place. Ferris's father liked to read the encyclopedia in his off-hours.

"It's certainly tempting to just leave her there," said Ferris's mother. She slammed another Green Stamp into the book. Boomer wagged his tail again.

Ferris's father turned slowly. He had a plum in his left hand and the encyclopedia in his right hand. "Now wait a minute," he said.

"What happened?" said Ferris.

"Your sister," said her mother, "attempted to rob Buford Milford Savings and Loan."

"Is Pinky old enough to rob a bank?" said Ferris.

"Your sister is old beyond her years," said Ferris's father. "She is incalculably old."

Incalculably.

A Mielk vocabulary word.

It meant in an extreme way, unable to be measured.

Yes, that seemed like a good word to apply to anything to do with Pinky.

"We're going to have to go down there and get her," said her mother.

Ferris's father sat down at the table. He took a bite of the plum. The afternoon light suddenly shone more brightly; the yellow table became incandescent.

It was very quiet in the kitchen. It was so quiet that you could hear Uncle Ted below them in the basement. You could hear him not painting the history of the world.

Ferris's father chewed the plum. That's how quiet it was. You could hear someone chew a plum.

Charisse was upstairs, asleep.

She slept all the time now. Or that was how it seemed to Ferris.

"I'm afraid," said Ferris into the plum-chewing silence. She couldn't have said exactly what she was afraid of – Charisse sleeping so much? The history of the world not getting painted? Pinky in the hands of the law? The law in the hands of Pinky?

"There's nothing to be afraid of, Ferris," said her mother. "It's just life. It's just learning to live in the world." She slid her chair back and stood up. "Well, who wants to go to the police station with me?"

Ferris's father sighed. He studied the pit of his plum, turning it slowly in his hand. "I have to go back to the office. I've got a meeting with Fred Tipton."

Ferris said, "I'll go, I guess. Let me check on Charisse first."

She climbed the stairs with Boomer following her. She could feel his hot breath on the back of her legs. It was comforting.

The door to Charisse's room was open. Ferris stood in the doorway and looked at Charisse sleeping. She was on her back. Her hands were folded on her chest and she was smiling.

Boomer went into the room and put his head on the bed, close to Charisse's face, and wagged his tail.

Charisse opened one eye.

"It's been so good," she said.

"What has?" said Ferris.

Charisse opened the other eye.

"All of it," she said.

"Pinky's been arrested," said Ferris.

"My goodness," said Charisse.

"She tried to rob a bank," said Ferris.

"Of course she did, darling," said Charisse.

"We're going to the police station to pick her up."

"Lovely," said Charisse. "I do so look forward to hearing the details." She closed her eyes.

Boomer wagged his tail some more, and then he lay down on the floor next to the bed with a thump and a sigh.

"Go on now," said Charisse with her eyes still closed. "Boomer will watch over me, and when you come back you can tell me about it – all the details. You're so good at details, darling. Pay attention now. Pay attention for me."

11

The police station smelt like carbon paper and staplers and also fertilizer because the sheriff was a man named Dale Percal who owned and managed the Percal Fertilizer company. When Ferris and her mother walked through the door, Dale Percal was sitting at his desk in front of a nameplate that said SHERRIFF PERCAL.

It was unnerving to Ferris to see that the word *sheriff* had been misspelt. Mrs Mielk insisted that being a good speller was the way to let people know your writing was trustworthy, that *you* were trustworthy. Shouldn't a sheriff be trustworthy?

"Hello," said Ferris's mother. "I'm Sarah Wilkey, here for Pinky."

Sheriff Percal shook his head slowly from side to side.

He said, "Mrs Wilkey, I got to tell you the truth. I have never in my life met anyone so unrepentant."

Unrepentant.

Not regretful.

Well, yes. That was another good word to apply to Pinky.

Ferris's mother sighed. She turned her head and looked out of the small window to the left of the sheriff's desk. The window was covered in chicken wire, which made it hard to see much of anything.

Sheriff Percal cleared his throat. He picked up the stapler from his desk and looked at it like he had never seen it before. "The question she kept asking me," he said as he studied the stapler, "was would she get her picture on a Wanted poster. And I told her it sure was likely. But that was before I figured out what she wanted. It's hard to understand her with those missing teeth, but I did finally understand. Yes, I did. She *wants* her face on a Wanted poster! Heaven help us, that's what she wants!"

The sheriff shook his head again and carefully placed the stapler back on the desk.

Ferris looked around the office. She wondered where Pinky was. Was she in an actual jail cell? Was she literally behind bars?

"Once I told her that it would never happen," continued the sheriff in his mournful and disbelieving voice, "once I convinced her that she would *not* get herself on a Wanted poster, well … then she started confessing other crimes to me, besides the, um, attempted bank robbery."

"What other crimes?" said Ferris's mother.

"Biting a nurse named Marla Dean, for one. Also, she confessed to stealing a pair of pliers from Mr Buoy down there at Buoy Hardware."

"Are you kidding me?" said Ferris's mother.

"I am not," said Sheriff Percal. "Now, what I have done is write this up." He picked up a pile of papers and shook them. "This is a police report, see? An official police report. I have typed it all up: the nurse-biting, the pliers, the stick-up at the bank and so on."

"Stick-up!" said Ferris's mother.

"That was the word she used," said the sheriff. "That was her exact word. So I put that in there along with the pliers and the nurse, and I made it look official. What I'm going to do is have you sign this paperwork, and then I'm going to release her to you and maybe the whole thing will have made an impression on her. Although I doubt it."

"I doubt it too," said Ferris's mother. "Where do I sign?"

"Here," said the sheriff. He cleared his throat. He pointed at the paper and then he turned his head and looked out of the window as if he was embarrassed by it all.

Ferris's mother signed the paper and stepped back, away from the desk. She opened her handbag and looked inside it and then closed it with a snap. She said, "She has always been a difficult child."

"I do not doubt it," said Sheriff Percal. He looked at Ferris. "This one seems law-abiding, though."

"Yes," said her mother. "She is. But being a rule follower carries its own set of problems."

It was true that Ferris never broke the rules.

Other than being born at the fair.

Which had surprised everybody and got written up in the paper. The headline was BABY MAKES DRAMATIC ENTRANCE AT THE FAIR.

"It was dramatic," her mother always said. "That's for sure."

Sheriff Percal stood up. "I'll go get her now. I wanted to give her some time back there to consider how she could maybe change her ways, but I'm guessing not much progress has been made in that regard."

"Right," said Ferris's mother.

The sheriff hitched up his trousers, squared his shoulders and walked down the hallway.

Ferris looked over at her mother. "How is being a rule follower a problem?" she asked.

"It's only that you're so eager to please people," said her mother, "and so tenderhearted. And the world—"

The sentence did not get finished because Pinky appeared in the hallway like a sudden storm cloud. She ran past them, her cape flying behind her, and went out of the door of the police station.

The sheriff handed Ferris's mother a copy of the police report.

"Thank you," she said. "We'll do our best not to show up here again."

"See if maybe you can get her to return the pliers to Mr Buoy," said Sheriff Percal.

"We'll do that. Among other things."

Ferris grabbed her mother's hand as they walked out of the police station.

It's only that you're so eager to please people and so tenderhearted. And the world...

What was the rest of that sentence?

That was what Ferris wanted to know.

Actually, there were a lot of things that Ferris wanted to know.

12

On the way home from the police station they passed Big Billy Jackson's Steakhouse and Ferris said, "Can I get out here?"

Her mother pulled into the empty parking lot and stopped the car. "I would get out here too if I could."

"Goodbye," said Ferris. "Good luck." She closed the door carefully.

Pinky glared at her from the back seat. She was sitting with her arms folded across her chest, muttering to herself.

After the car left, Ferris stood in the parking lot and listened. She could hear piano music.

Billy Jackson.

The steakhouse didn't open until five o'clock,

and Billy Jackson spent most afternoons in its dimly lit interior, practising the piano. When the restaurant opened for dinner, a man named Bob Munson played the piano while people ate.

Mr Munson was bald except for a fringe of hair around his ears. Every night, he wore the same outfit: a ruffled tuxedo shirt and black trousers that had a satin stripe down the side of them. He played songs like "Moon River" and "My Funny Valentine" and kept a goldfish bowl on top of the piano. At the beginning of the night, Mr Munson put a few dollar bills into the bowl "to give people a little kick in the pants and point them in the right direction".

When Bob Munson played the piano, he got sweaty. He kept a towel on the piano bench and he had to stop in between songs to wipe the sweat off his upper lip and the top of his head.

Mr Munson called Billy Jackson "Billy the Kid".

He said, "Billy the Kid here thinks he's a real piano player. Well, we'll see if he's got what it takes. The world knocks the stuffing out of piano players.

Have you noticed that? Huh? Real piano players don't last long in this world."

Bob Munson kept his eyes on the fishbowl full of dollar bills while he played. Sometimes he nodded at it in an encouraging way.

Ferris opened the door to the steakhouse and was met by a blue haze of cigarette smoke. The smoke was from the night before – from all the nights before. It lingered.

Crumbs lingered too.

Boomer loved to visit the steakhouse when it was closed. He would move from booth to booth and table to table, looking for french fries and breadcrumbs and also errant butter patties, which he would swallow whole, foil and all. Sometimes, Boomer found a small piece of steak. When this happened, he emitted a single low woof – a deeply satisfied noise of surprise and delight.

Ferris walked across the red carpet (everything in the steakhouse was red: the glass candle holders and the Naugahyde booths and the tablecloths; even the windows were made of a pebbled red glass). All the way at the back of the room, Billy Jackson was playing the piano.

"Hey, Ferris," he said.

On the wall behind the piano was a big poster-sized picture of Billy Jackson's mother, who was dead, who had died giving birth to Billy.

This was a tragedy, of course.

But in the gigantic picture of her, Billy Jackson's mother looked happy. She had a big, floppy white hat on her head, and she had her hands on either side of the hat, as if she was trying to keep it on her head in a strong wind. She was standing in a field of tall grass and she was smiling into the camera, and you couldn't help but smile back at her. She was beautiful.

"Where's Boomer?" Billy Jackson said to Ferris, still playing the piano.

"He's at home," said Ferris, "watching over Charisse."

Ferris could hear the solid *thwack, thwack, thwack* of a knife on a cutting board – Big Billy was chopping vegetables in the kitchen. Sometimes when Big Billy was prepping for dinner, he would take a break and come out into the dining room and sit down in a (red) chair and put his gigantic hands on his knees and look at Billy Jackson playing the piano and also at the picture of Billy's mother standing in the tall grass, working to keep her hat on her head.

Big Billy would just sit there and smile at both of them – his piano-playing son and his dead wife.

"Pinky got arrested," said Ferris to Billy Jackson.

Billy stopped playing the piano.

"Arrested?" he said. His glasses slipped down his nose and he pushed them back in place with his index finger.

"It was more like a pretend arrest," said Ferris. "To try and scare her."

"What did she do?" said Billy.

The sun coming in through the pebbled windows was making tiny red rectangles that landed on the piano keys and on Billy Jackson's hands. The pieces of light looked like confetti that someone had tossed around the room.

Sometimes Ferris felt as if the red-hued,

smoke-filled restaurant was some kind of magic trick – a place conjured into existence by an ambitious magician.

"She tried to rob Buford Milford Savings and Loan," said Ferris.

"A bank robber," said Billy Jackson in a thoughtful voice. "Pinky Wilkey, the infamous bank robber."

Infamous meant being well known for a bad deed.

There were so many Mielk vocabulary words that applied to Pinky!

"Also, she stole a pair of pliers from Buoy Hardware."

Billy Jackson smiled. He shook his head. "The Infamous Pinky Wilkey," he said. And then he went back to playing the piano.

"She drives me crazy," said Ferris. "She is unfathomable."

Billy Jackson nodded. He said, "Yeah, Pinky is kind of hard to understand. But you could maybe ask her what she is thinking."

Ferris sat down on the bench next to Billy Jackson.

A big clatter came out of the kitchen. "Dang it, now!" shouted Big Billy. "Gosh dang it."

Billy Jackson kept playing the piano.

The first time Ferris had come to the steakhouse, the very first time, she had been only six years old, and Big Billy had come out of the kitchen wearing a stained white apron and holding a knife. He looked like a giant out of a fairy tale. He stood with his hands on his hips and stared at Ferris, and she almost expected him to say *Fee, fie, fo, fum!*

Instead he had said, "Is that Ferris Wilkey I see before me?"

"Yes, sir," she told him. "It's me."

"Well, now," said Big Billy. "Ferris Wilkey, are you the kind of child who likes pie?"

"Yes, sir," said Ferris.

"Do you like your pie à la mode?"

"I don't know that that means," she told him.

"It means a piece of pie with some ice cream melting on top of it!" Big Billy shouted. "Do you want that?"

"Yes, sir, I do!" Ferris had shouted back.

Big Billy Jackson appeared now out of the smoky magician's air, wearing his dirty apron and smiling.

He stood and looked at Ferris sitting next to Billy on the piano bench.

"What happened to your hair, Ferris Wilkey?" he said.

"It's a long story," she told him.

"Well, all right, then. Do you think you could eat you some pie à la mode while you tell it to me?"

"Yes, sir," she told him. "I could."

13

When Ferris got home, it was almost supper time. Pinky was in her bedroom. The police report was nailed to her door. The many pages of it rustled in the breeze blowing in through the open window at the end of the hall.

Unfathomable.

Incapable of being understood.

Ferris stood in front of Pinky's closed door and thought about Billy Jackson saying that she could ask Pinky what she was thinking. But if she did that, Pinky would probably laugh in her face and tell her that her hair looked funny. What was the point?

So instead Ferris walked on down the hallway, which was like walking down a tunnel of roses because the walls were covered in wallpaper that was all red roses and thorny branches. Some of the roses had faded to a ghostly pink from the sun beating in on them for years and years.

In Charisse's room, Charisse was sitting at her desk with a sweater over her shoulders even though it was hot out. She was writing something.

The sweet, hopeful smell of Florida water filled the room. It made Ferris's heart hurt.

"Pinky got locked up in a jail cell," said Ferris.

"So I have been informed, darling," said Charisse.

"What are you writing?"

"Instructions."

"Instructions for what?" said Ferris. "Where's Boomer?"

"He left," said Charisse. "Right before the ghost appeared, he slunk away – as is his wont. Something extraordinary has happened, darling."

"Yes," said Ferris. "Pinky tried to rob a bank."

Charisse waved her hand through the air. "No, no, not that," she said. "The ghost spoke, darling. The ghost spoke to me."

Ferris shivered. "She *talked* to you?"

"She did. I know what she wants."

"What?" said Ferris. "What does she want?"

Boomer appeared at the threshold of Charisse's room. He barked once, looking right at Ferris, and then he came into the room sideways, wagging his tail in an embarrassed way.

"I'll tell you after supper," said Charisse. "It really was the most extraordinary conversation."

That night, both Pinky and Ted were missing from the supper table. Billy Jackson didn't show up either.

It was just Charisse and Ferris and Boomer and Ferris's mother and father.

"Pinky is under house arrest," said her mother. "I'm devising a program for her rehabilitation."

"Miscreants of all sorts abound in this house," said Ferris's father. "I think we might need to contact an exterminator to deal with the raccoon problem."

"But wouldn't an exterminator kill them?" said Ferris.

"Speaking of the dead," said Charisse. "I have

had an extremely straightforward communication from the beyond."

"Beyond what?" said Ferris's mother.

Charisse looked up at the chandelier. She was smiling.

Ferris's father looked up at the chandelier too.

"It's going to be glorious," said Charisse.

"What is?" said Ferris's mother.

Ferris bent her head back and looked up at the old chandelier.

"What are you people looking at?" said Ferris's mother.

"I'm not certain," said Ferris's father.

Charisse, without lowering her head, reached over and put her hand on top of Ferris's hand.

After supper, Ferris and Boomer followed Charisse up to her room.

Ferris sat down in the window. Charisse sat on the edge of the bed and Boomer threw himself down at her feet.

"You have to tell me," said Ferris.

"It has to do with the chandelier," said Charisse.

"What about it?"

"The ghost wants it lit. It has never been lit, you see. Not once. Her husband went off to war before the chandelier was even hung. And then he did not come back."

"He died?"

"Yes," said Charisse. "He died without ever seeing it. The chandelier was a gift for his wife. He had it specially ordered from Paris. And when he did not return from the war, she – the ghost, his wife – refused to let anyone ever light the chandelier. She was just too brokenhearted. She would not let candles anywhere near it. And she regrets it now. She is consumed with regret."

"Why?" said Ferris.

"Because she can't find him, darling. She is searching for him and can't find him. She believes that if the chandelier is lit, he will find his way to her."

Ferris looked down at her arms. The hair on them was standing up.

Boomer was panting. He looked nervous. He couldn't possibly have understood what Charisse had just said; Ferris barely understood it. But still, Boomer seemed deeply unnerved.

"Darling," said Charisse. "I need you to help me."

"What should I do?" said Ferris.

"I counted at supper," said Charisse. "We need forty candles."

"Forty," repeated Ferris.

"And a ladder," said Charisse.

"And a ladder," said Ferris.

"Yes," said Charisse. "We're going to light the chandelier, darling. We're going to help someone find their way home."

14

Ferris played gin rummy with Charisse and then she read aloud to her from the Bible (*"for you are dust, and to dust you will return"*) and Whitman (*"I bequeath myself to the dirt to grow from the grass I love"*) and Charisse clapped her hands and said, "Dust and dirt, darling! There's a theme!" Ferris thought it was a pretty depressing theme.

Afterwards, she went down to the steakhouse and climbed the rusty ladder to the roof.

Billy Jackson was waiting for her.

"You know who came in tonight?" he said as soon as she stepped onto the roof.

"No," said Ferris.

"Mrs Mielk," said Billy Jackson.

"Really?" said Ferris.

"Yeah," said Billy Jackson. "Really." He had his arms wrapped around his knees and he was looking up at the sky. "She was by herself, and she ordered a hamburger and ate it with a knife and fork instead of picking it up with her hands, and for dessert Pop brought her a piece of peach pie à la mode.

"He said, 'This here is on the house in honour of all the words you have given to my son and his friend Ferris Wilkey.' Because I had told Pop about how you and me felt about those Mielk words – that it was terrible to memorize them but good to have them, and how, in the end, we felt grateful to her. I had told that to Pop."

Billy Jackson lowered his head and looked at Ferris. "So Pop thanked her, and then he put the pie down on the table in front of her and Mrs Mielk started to cry."

"Mrs Mielk cried?"

"Yeah," said Billy. "I was in the kitchen with Pearl, and Pop came in there and he said to me, 'Son, go out into the dining room and set with your teacher while she eats her pie. She's crying.'"

"And you went?"

"Well," said Billy. "Pop asked me to."

"Did she eat the pie?"

"She did."

"Did she say anything to you?"

Billy Jackson shook his head. "No," he said. His glasses caught the light of the steakhouse sign and flashed bright in the darkness. "She just kept crying and ate her pie."

"And she was all by herself?"

"Yeah," said Billy Jackson.

"That's weird," said Ferris. She sat down on the roof. The asphalt was warm beneath her. From down below she could hear Boomer panting hopefully. Pearl was slamming things around in the kitchen, and from what seemed like a really long way away came the sound of Bob Munson playing the piano – the theme from Dr Zhivago.

Ferris thought about Mrs Mielk sitting by herself eating peach pie à la mode and crying. It was disturbing. There must be a word to describe a story like that, but what would it be?

Haunting.

That was probably the best word.

Haunting meant evocative, unforgettable.

The image of Billy Jackson's mother holding on to her hat and smiling and happy was haunting too. Ferris thought about how when the steakhouse was empty, when no one else was there, Billy's mother was still there, like a ghost, standing in the tall grass, smiling.

"Do you ever think about your mother?" Ferris said to Billy Jackson.

And then she was ashamed that she had never thought to ask him the question before.

Billy said, "It's not that I think about her. It's more like she's always with me." He was quiet. Ferris waited. Even when they weren't talking about something big and important, Billy Jackson took a long time between sentences.

"Big thinker, slow talker" was how Uncle Ted described him.

Ferris had learned to wait.

"You know how you swear you can remember

seeing Charisse's face when you were born?" said Billy.

Ferris nodded.

"And everyone tells you how that's not possible? That there is no way you can remember?"

"Yes," said Ferris.

"Well, I can remember my mother. I remember her singing to me."

"But from when?" said Ferris.

"From before I was even born," said Billy. "I can feel her hand on me, resting on me, and I can hear her singing. I don't ever tell Pop about it because I think it would make him too sad. I don't know."

There was another long silence.

Ferris waited.

"Anyway," said Billy Jackson. "I think that's where the music comes from. From her singing to me. And that's why I don't feel lonely for her. Because she's here all the time. In the music."

Ferris nodded. She wanted to say something that let Billy know she understood.

"Every story is a love story," she said.

"Yeah," said Billy. "That."

Below them, Boomer barked a joyful bark and Pearl said, "You big old mess of a dog. You think you're getting a bone?"

"The ghost talked to Charisse," said Ferris.

Billy Jackson nodded. "Everyone talks to Charisse."

"She wants the chandelier lit. I mean, the ghost wants the chandelier lit. And Charissc wants it too."

"Why?" said Billy.

"So that her husband can find his way back home. We need forty candles and a ladder."

The screen door creaked open, and Pearl said to Boomer, "Here it is, you big old mess. Here's your bone. I don't know why you think you deserve all this love."

The screen door banged shut.

Billy Jackson smiled. "Forty candles and a ladder. That sounds like something we can do."

Ferris felt her heart contract with gratitude.

She loved Billy Jackson.

She loved Boomer.

She loved Pearl.

She loved the sound of the screen door opening and closing.

She loved the roof of the steakhouse and the stars shining over her head, over all their heads.

"Every story is a love story," whispered Ferris. "Every good story is a love story."

15

Pinky was in the paper the next day.

According to the article, a "young child in a black cloak" had gone unaccompanied into the Buford Milford Savings and Loan and approached the desk of Irene Milford.

"I thought the child was a trick-or-treater," Mrs Milford was quoted as saying. "I guess I lost track of my seasons. In any case, she resembled a vampire of some sort. And so I started looking for some candy."

Apparently Mrs Milford had dug around in the top drawer of her desk until she located a piece of butterscotch.

"But alas," the article ended, "the offer of a single butterscotch candy enraged the child, and it was at this point that she started screaming about how she was attempting to rob the bank. Eventually it became necessary to call the police."

Ferris's father read the words aloud in a tone of awe.

They were in the kitchen – Ferris, her mother, her father, Boomer.

It was morning, and sunlight was shining on the glossy leaves of the magnolia tree, and Ferris was drinking coffee again.

"My goodness," said Ferris's father when he had done reading. "Well." He cleared his throat. "I suppose it's nice to have such a full accounting of what happened, what with Pinky herself being unwilling to disclose any details."

Ferris's mother was sitting at the kitchen table with her hands in her lap. She was staring straight ahead. "I really don't know what to do with her," she said.

"Ted was a bit of a wild child," said Ferris's father.

"Yes," said her mother, still staring straight ahead, "and where is he now?"

"In the basement."

"Exactly."

"Can I have the newspaper?" said Ferris. "I want to read it to Charisse."

"I doubt it will help her heart any," said Ferris's mother.

Ferris stood up and took the paper from her father's outstretched hand.

Boomer stood up too. He wagged his tail. He looked in the direction of the pantry, and then he looked at the door to the basement, and then he looked back at the pantry again. Clearly Boomer was hoping that Ferris would get some peanuts and take them down to Uncle Ted.

Which was a good idea.

She and Billy Jackson were going to need help lighting the chandelier.

They needed an adult, a quixotic adult.

Quixotic meant exceedingly unrealistic and foolish, like someone who would quit their job to paint the history of the world.

In other words, someone like Uncle Ted.

"Actually," said Ferris, "I think I'll go show Uncle Ted the article first."

She went to the pantry and got out the jar of peanuts. Boomer wagged his tail faster.

"If Ted wants peanuts," said her mother, "why doesn't he come up here and get them himself?"

"The way I look at it," said her father, "is that we should eat everything we can before the raccoons take over the house and beat us to the punch."

"The raccoons have already taken over the house," said her mother. "Metaphorically speaking."

Ferris went down the basement steps carefully, the newspaper under one arm, the jar of peanuts in both hands and Boomer close at her heels.

"Uncle Ted?" she called.

Ted, unshaven and still in his bathrobe, appeared at the bottom of the stairs, smiling up at her.

"I brought you some peanuts," said Ferris. "I still feel bad for telling Aunt Shirley about the foot."

"Ah," said Ted. "The peanuts of repentance. Thank you, honey."

He took the jar from her and unscrewed the lid

and poured a stream of peanuts into his mouth.

Boomer barked. Ted tossed him a peanut.

"Are you growing a beard?" said Ferris.

"I am," said Ted. "It gives me a certain painterly gravitas, don't you think?"

"I don't know. What's gravitas?"

"It means dignity, honey. Something I am in dire need of right now."

Ferris thought the beard made Ted look less like a dignified painter and more like a prophet lost in the desert.

"Come on over here," said Ted, "and I will show you how I have progressed. I am painting the second foot."

Ferris walked over to the canvas and stood beside Uncle Ted.

The second foot was at a good distance from the first, but it was similar-looking – lumpy, disembodied.

"That's good," said Ferris. She thought for a while about what to say next. "Do you know, um, who the feet belong to?"

Uncle Ted stared at the canvas. "Not yet," he said. "I'm sure it will come to me."

Ferris handed him the newspaper. She said, "There's an article in there about Pinky. It doesn't use her name but it's definitely her. I thought you might want to read it."

Ted put down the peanut jar. He took the paper and snapped it open and held it out and away from him. He read with a serious look on his face until he got to the butterscotch.

"'But alas,'" Uncle Ted read aloud, "'the offer of a single butterscotch candy enraged the child.'"

He started to laugh. He laughed so hard that he had to bend over and put his hands on his knees.

Uncle Ted in his bathrobe with his hair sticking straight up and peanut crumbs on his face and tears of laughter rolling down his cheeks and into his prophet beard was an unsettling sight.

Boomer barked at him in a scolding way.

Ted stood up. "Wheeeeee," he said. He wiped at his eyes. "Thank you, honey. I don't know when a newspaper has cheered me up more." He handed the paper back to Ferris. "And I do need to laugh. Yes, I surely do. For my poor heart is broken."

"Because of Shirley?" said Ferris.

"Yes, honey. Because of Shirley. I find that I cannot live without her. She's necessary to me."

Ferris thought about Shirley – frosted and sparkling, small and twirling. Nothing about her seemed particularly necessary.

"Who can explain the human heart?" said Ted.

Oh, hearts.

Charisse's heart.

"Charisse is taking those pills Dr Trench gave her," Ferris said. "But I don't think she feels that good. She sleeps and sleeps. I'm worried."

Uncle Ted smiled at her. "Honey." He put his hands on her shoulders, one hand on each shoulder. It was the same way Reverend Mulberry put his hands on her when he blessed her in the communion line.

The smell of peanuts and bathrobe and oil paints filled the air.

Boomer wagged his tail.

Uncle Ted looked deep into Ferris's eyes. He said, "I don't understand any of it. I truly don't. The world is a mystery to me. But yet here we are, and our hearts keep on beating. They keep wanting things, don't they?"

Which wasn't really a blessing.

But still, it managed to seem like one to Ferris because it gave her a way to talk about Charisse and the ghost.

She said, "Uncle Ted, Charisse has been seeing a ghost."

"Lordy," said Uncle Ted.

"And the ghost talked to her."

"I see," said Ted. "Please continue."

"The ghost wants something."

Ted nodded. "Uh-huh." He kept his hands on her shoulders.

"Charisse said the ghost wants the old chandelier lit. I'm going to get the candles, and Billy Jackson is going to help. Forty candles. We can do that part. But the ladder and the matches and the lighting … we'll need an adult for that."

"So what this ghost wants is more light?" said Ted.

"Yes," said Ferris.

"That's just exactly my kind of project," said Ted. His hands were still on her shoulders. He was smiling, and Ferris smiled back at him.

Boomer pushed his way in between them, wagging his tail furiously, whacking Ferris in the knees.

"More light," said Uncle Ted. "That's what we're all about around here. More light is good."

16

I'll tell you what's going to happen," said Ferris's mother when Ferris and Boomer came back up from the basement. "We're going to work to set Pinky on a different path. That's what's going to happen."

Ferris's father had left for the office, and outside the kitchen window the birds were singing a complicated morning song. There was a blue jay in the branches of the magnolia tree.

"Sit down," said her mother.

Ferris sat down.

"First," said her mother, "we're going to get Pinky her own library card."

"OK," said Ferris.

"After the library, we'll go to Buoy Hardware and have Pinky apologize to Mr Buoy and return the pliers."

Futile.

That was the Mielk vocabulary word that seemed to apply to this plan of her mother's.

It was pointless to try and reform Pinky.

Besides, Ferris had other, more important things to tend to – like candles and ladders and ghosts. She opened her mouth to say so.

"No," said her mother. "She's your sister. You're coming with me."

"OK," said Ferris.

It was also futile to argue with her mother.

When it was time to leave, Pinky came down the stairs without her cloak. She was wearing a pair of red shorts and a blue-striped top. Her hair was combed. She looked almost normal.

Ferris wasn't fooled, though.

"Where's your cape?" said Ferris.

"None of your bithneth," said Pinky. "Leth go."

🦋 🦋 🦋

Thelma Atkins was the head librarian at the Bingham Memorial Library. Mrs Atkins had a gold-plated tag pinned to her blouse that read MRS ATKINS, HEAD LIBRARIAN. Mrs Atkins wore her glasses on a chain around her neck, but Ferris had never seen her actually put the glasses on. It was more like they were for decoration.

"Good morning, Thelma," said Ferris's mother. "We're here to get Pinky a library card."

"Who?" said Mrs Atkins.

Mrs Atkins did not approve of nicknames, and she would not put them on library cards. Ferris's library card read EMMA WILKEY. Sometimes when Ferris looked at it she wondered who it belonged to.

"Eleanor Rose," said Ferris's mother. "We're here for a library card for Eleanor Rose." She pushed Pinky forward, towards Mrs Atkins.

"How old are you, dear?" said Mrs Atkins.

"Thickth," said Pinky.

"Well, now," said Mrs Atkins. She bent down and put her hands on her knees and looked Pinky in the eye.

Ferris felt like this was probably a mistake.

"Six years old," said Mrs Atkins, "is not old enough

for a library card. In my library you have to be able to *read* to acquire a library card. And you, my dear, will learn how to do that when you attend first grade."

"I can read now," said Pinky in a voice of deadly calm.

"It's true," said Ferris's mother. "She taught herself. Somehow. When she was four."

Mrs Atkins stood up. She released a disbelieving breath through her nostrils. "Well," she said. "We'll see about that, won't we?" She turned and pulled a thick book off a library cart: Hans Christian Andersen's *Complete Fairy Tales*. Mrs Atkins flipped through the volume until she found a particular page.

"Now then," she said to Pinky. She handed her the book. "Why don't you read that to me?"

It was the story of the little match girl, and Pinky read it through without stumbling or hesitating. True, some of the words sounded funny because of Pinky's missing teeth, but she knew every word.

Ferris's mother had edged away and was looking at the new arrivals display, but Ferris stood transfixed as Pinky read.

Transfixed.

Frozen in horror or astonishment.

Because who knew what was going to happen in the showdown between Mrs Atkins and Pinky?

Pinky slammed the book shut when she was done reading. "Thath *that* thtory," she said.

"My goodness," said Mrs Atkins, who looked impressed but unwilling to admit it.

"That girl thould have juth robbed a bank," said Pinky.

"I beg your pardon?" said Mrs Atkins.

"That thilly girl thould have robbed a bank!" said Pinky. "She thould have done thumpthing to rethcue herthelf."

"Well," said Mrs Atkins. "Perhaps."

And then, for the first time ever, Ferris saw Mrs Atkins raise her glasses up to her eyes. She did it so she could study Pinky. She stared at her as if she was a particularly interesting specimen of some sort.

"That girl should have *acted*," said Pinky.

Mrs Atkins rocked back on her heels. She lowered the glasses. She said, "I would be happy to issue a library card to such an excellent reader and, um, original thinker. Would you like some assistance in selecting your books?"

"Maybe," said Pinky. She crossed her arms over her chest and stared somewhere past Thelma Atkins.

Ferris had to admit that she felt just the tiniest bit proud to know Pinky. Talk about formidable.

In the end, Pinky left with two non-fiction books – one about deadly snakes and the other about Houdini. Ferris checked out *Anne of Green Gables*, even though she had already read it, and her mother selected a biography of Abraham Lincoln in an effort to "shore up her moral fortitude".

"Speaking of moral fortitude," said her mother. "We will now go to Buoy Hardware. Pinky, you will go in there and return those pliers and issue an apology."

Pinky said nothing. She was studying a full-page picture of a rattlesnake in her *Snakes You Do Not Want to Meet!* book.

When they arrived at Buoy Hardware, Pinky walked into the store without complaint. She marched up to the counter and pulled the pliers from the pocket of her shorts and handed them to Mr Buoy.

"What's this?" said Mr Buoy, taking the pliers from her.

"I thtole them," said Pinky.

"How's that?" said Mr Buoy. He fiddled with his hearing aid.

"I THTOLE THEM!" shouted Pinky.

"Thank you so much," said Mr Buoy. "Whatever you're saying, I appreciate it very much. What a handsome pair of pliers."

"I'm thorry," said Pinky.

"She said she's sorry," said Ferris's mother in a very loud voice. "She stole the pliers and used them to pull a few of her own teeth. Which is why it's difficult to understand her."

"Heavens," said Mr Buoy. "That must have hurt."

Pinky shrugged.

Mr Buoy winked at her. He bent down and disappeared below the counter, and then he slowly reappeared holding three lollipops – a red one and a green one and a yellow one.

He handed the red lollipop to Pinky. "All is forgiven," said Mr Buoy.

He held out the green and yellow lollipops to Ferris and said, "Here you go, my dear. I remember when you were born."

"You do?" said Ferris.

"Yes, indeed. I was at the fair that day. It was all very exciting."

"It sure was," said Ferris's mother.

Ferris reached out to take the lollipops from Mr Buoy. He wrapped his warm and calloused hand around her fingers and pulled her closer. "If you wouldn't mind, could you give this other one, the yellow one, to your grandmother from me?"

"You want me to give a lollipop to Charisse?" said Ferris.

"Yes," said Mr Buoy. "Please. She has been breaking hearts since the day she came into the world. She has certainly broken mine. Give her my love."

Ferris's mother sighed loudly. "Thank you, Mr Buoy," she said. "I'm sorry for the inconvenience."

Mr Buoy waved his hand through the air dismissively.

"It's all inconvenience," he said. "And then suddenly it's over. And you find yourself thinking that you wouldn't mind a little inconvenience."

Pinky exited the hardware store. The door shut behind her with a loud bang.

"Do you sell candles?" Ferris said to Mr Buoy.

"How's that?" said Mr Buoy.

"Candles!" shouted Ferris. "Lights!"

"We sell flashlights, patio lights and lanterns," said Mr Buoy.

Ferris's mother turned to her and said, "What in the world do you need candles for?" And this was when Ferris realized, for the first time, that the chandelier wasn't going to get lit without her mother's approval.

"Go on and give that lollipop to Charisse," said Mr Buoy. "Promise me you will, now."

"I promise," said Ferris.

"Give it to her with my regards," said Mr Buoy, "and also my love."

17

That night after supper, Pinky locked herself in her room with her library books. The police report was gone from her door. It had been replaced with a sign that said: "Studying. DO NOT DISTURB."

Ferris thought about knocking on Pinky's door and telling her that she admired how formidable she had been with Mrs Atkins. But the sign said "DO NOT DISTURB", and it was probably a good idea – in general – not to disturb Pinky.

Charisse was in her room playing solitaire on the bed.

"Here," said Ferris. She held out the yellow lollipop. "I forgot to give you this. Mr Buoy sent it to you with his regards and his love. That's what he told me to tell you."

"Allen Buoy!" Charisse said. She clapped her hands in delight. "Is that man still carrying a torch for me?" She unwrapped the lollipop. "Speaking of torches, what about the chandelier lighting?"

"It's kind of complicated," said Ferris. "Billy Jackson is going to help me, and so is Uncle Ted. But I have to tell Mom and Dad about it. I think I'm going to have to get permission."

"Oh, pooh, permission!" said Charisse. She held out the lollipop and studied it, turning it from side to side. "We must not let ourselves be deterred, Emmaphineas. What I mean by that is: don't let your mother talk you out of it. She errs on the side of sensibleness, which is not always the best side to err on."

"OK," said Ferris. "I'm going to talk to them now. I'll let you know how it goes."

She found her parents on the front porch, sitting together on the porch swing.

Ferris's mother was reading about the life of Lincoln and Ferris's father was reading the *J–K* volume of the encyclopedia. Part of the reason her father read random volumes of the encyclopedia was that he liked to be surprised; he liked to encounter the unexpected.

Ferris's mother said that "an appetite for the unexpected" was the Achilles heel of all the Wilkeys.

Achilles heel was a Mielk vocabulary word.

Even though it was more like a phrase.

It meant a weakness, a vulnerability.

"Hey Ferris," said her father when she walked onto the porch. He pushed against the porch floor with one foot so that the swing rocked back and forth gently. He didn't look up from the encyclopedia.

"Hey," said Ferris back.

"Hmmm," said her father. "Who knew?"

"Shhh," said her mother.

"Fascinating," said her father. He gave the swing another push.

"Did you need something, Ferris?" said her mother. She turned a page in the Lincoln book.

Ferris stood and looked at her parents.

The crickets were singing.

Billy Jackson had told Ferris once that everything

in the whole world made music. The trees made music and the stones made music and so did the flowers and the grass and the grains of sand.

"The whole world is singing all the time, and we don't even know it."

That was what Billy Jackson had said.

Ferris took a deep breath. "Charisse wants us to light the old chandelier."

Her parents both looked up from their books.

"What?" said her mother. "No."

"I don't think anyone has ever used that chandelier, honey," said her father. "It's just for show."

"It needs forty candles," said Ferris. "I'll get them, and Uncle Ted will help with the ladder and also the matches and the lighting. Billy Jackson will help too. It's for Charisse. It's what Charisse wants. She doesn't feel well, and it's what she wants."

She didn't say anything about the ghost and what the ghost wanted.

Ferris's mother closed the biography of Lincoln with a loud thump. She looked at Ferris. "So *this* is what the candles were about."

"It's a gift," said Ferris. "A gift for Charisse. Can't we do it, please?"

Boomer came out onto the porch and stood next to Ferris. He wagged his tail, hopefully, from side to side.

Ferris's mother sighed. "It's always something around here, isn't it?"

"Speaking of which," said her father. "I called the exterminator."

"Oh no," said Ferris.

Boomer stopped wagging his tail.

"We cannot simply hand over the house to the raccoons, honey," said her father.

"We can't agree to burn it down, either," said her mother.

"I bet it would be glorious to see that chandelier all lit up," said her father. "I bet it would be magical."

"You Wilkeys," said her mother. She shook her head. "You people."

"We'll be careful," said Ferris.

"Oh good grief," said her mother. "I give up. But listen to me. I want to be apprised every step of the way, and I do not want Pinky involved. I do not want this to turn into some incident that we will read about in the paper the next morning as we sit in the smouldering ruins of our house."

Ferris looked at the little white moths dancing and flittering around the porch light.

The moths were probably singing too.

"Ferris?" said her mother. "Promise me."

Ferris stood up straighter. "I promise."

It occurred to her that she had been making a lot of promises lately.

18

Mrs Mielk was bereft.

Bereft was a Mielk vocabulary word.

Something about the circular logic of this – Mrs Mielk having provided the right word for better understanding of how she, Mrs Mielk, felt – made Ferris slightly dizzy. It deepened the power of words, the power that Mrs Mielk had so often talked about, the lightning-like effect of them.

Bereft.

Robbed of the possession of something.

The something (or rather, someone) that Mrs Mielk had been robbed of was Mr Mielk.

"And she told you she was bereft?" said Ferris.

"No," said Billy Jackson. "But that's what she is."

They were in the steakhouse. It was afternoon

and Boomer was snuffling his way along the carpet, eating breadcrumbs and also the crumbs of other things. He was making happy sounds and wagging his tail to himself.

If Boomer ever thought about heaven, if he ever imagined what it would be like, Ferris thought that Big Billy Jackson's Steakhouse in the afternoon before the crumbs had been vacuumed up – Ferris sitting somewhere near by and Billy Jackson playing the piano – was probably what the dog would come up with.

"When Mrs Mielk came in last night," said Billy, "she didn't even order a burger. She just asked for some fries and then she sat and stared at them. Pop told me to go out there and sit with her again."

"Did she talk to you?"

"Mostly she just cried. Bob Munson was playing that song 'King of the Road'. You know that song?"

Billy switched from playing "Mysterious Barricades" to playing "King of the Road". After a few bars, he stopped and let his hands rest on the keys.

"Anyway," he said. "Mr Munson played that song,

and Mrs Mielk cried all the way through it, and then at the end she said to me how her husband had liked that song and how he'd whistled it all the time when he was out in the workshop repairing things. And then she said how futile it was to bother repairing things in this hopelessly broken world."

Ferris's mother had shown her the obituary in the paper that morning. There was a picture of Mr Mielk. He had on horn-rimmed glasses and a string tie, and it said below the picture that he liked fishing and had fought in the European theatre in World War II and that he was survived by his children, Pete and Nancy, and his wife of thirty-six years, Imogene.

Imogene.

Mrs Mielk's first name was Imogene.

It made Ferris's heart hurt.

Sitting at the kitchen table looking at the obituary, Ferris had told her mother how Mrs Mielk had come into the steakhouse and ordered a hamburger and eaten it with a knife and fork and cried and cried and how Billy Jackson had sat with her and how Mrs Mielk had not spoken at all. Mrs Mielk, who loved words so much, had been rendered mute.

"Grief does that," said her mother.

"Does what?" said Ferris.

"Takes away your words," said her mother. "At least for a while, it takes everything away."

But who would Mrs Mielk be without words? How could she even continue to be Mrs Mielk?

"Bereft," Ferris said to Billy Jackson. "It's a lonely word. It makes me think of a raft that has floated out to sea."

"Yeah," said Billy Jackson. "A raft where you're the only one on it." He started playing "Mysterious Barricades" again.

"I've got money for the candles," said Ferris. "Charisse gave it to me. I figure that we could go to Furnace Dime."

"Yes," said Billy Jackson. He kept playing. His face looked serious, thoughtful, and Ferris, watching him, heard Uncle Ted saying, "More light ... more light is good."

Furnace Dime was downtown next to Shirley Curl. The inside of the store smelt like mothballs and melted cheese, because Miss Furnace made grilled cheese sandwiches on a small griddle and sold them for fifty cents.

You could sit at a little counter in Furnace Dime and eat your grilled cheese and drink a cup of coffee and look out at Main Street. The day Pinky was born, Ferris and her father had come to the dime store and had grilled cheese sandwiches and looked out of the window together.

"Now you're a big sister," her father had said. "You have someone who will love you and look up to you. You have gained a lifetime companion. You have waded deeper into the great river of life."

Her father had let her take a sip of coffee from his cup, and Miss Furnace had told him that children shouldn't drink coffee because it stunted their growth.

"It would be impossible to stunt the growth of this child," said Ferris's father. "She has a sister. Together, they will grow and flourish."

That was what her father had said to Miss Furnace about Ferris and Pinky on the day that Pinky was born.

It made Ferris happy to remember it.

It also made her wish that Pinky was the kind of person who was less interested in deadly snakes and more interested in growing and flourishing.

"What do you children want?" said Miss Furnace when Ferris and Billy Jackson walked into the store.

Charisse had told Ferris that the chandelier required taper candles.

"We need taper candles," said Ferris.

"Taper candles?" said Miss Furnace. "What would a child like you possibly want with taper candles?"

"It's for a chandelier," said Billy Jackson.

"A chandelier at that steakhouse?" said Miss Furnace in a tone of outraged disbelief.

"It's for a chandelier at my house," said Ferris.

"Hmmpph," said Miss Furnace. She stared hard at Ferris. "You are Charisse Wilkey's granddaughter."

"Yes, ma'am," said Ferris.

"Shirley Wilkey is your aunt," said Miss Furnace.

"Yes, ma'am," said Ferris again.

"Did she do that to your hair?" said Miss Furnace.

There had been so much going on – failing hearts and talking ghosts, dead husbands and stolen pliers, police reports and attempted bank robberies – that Ferris had forgotten about her hair. She put a hand up and touched its frizzy strangeness.

"Yes, ma'am," she said. "She did."

"It looks ridiculous," said Miss Furnace.

"Ma'am," said Billy Jackson in an extremely polite voice, "what we need is forty taper candles."

"No one *needs* forty taper candles," said Miss Furnace.

"We do," said Ferris. "Charisse does."

"Charisse," said Miss Furnace. She said the name the way a snake might say it if a snake owned a dime store and could speak. "You may tell *Charisse* that the world, much as she supposes it to be, is not her oyster."

"OK," said Ferris, even though she wasn't sure what Miss Furnace was talking about.

Ferris's father had said to her that day six years ago when they sat eating their grilled cheese sandwiches in Furnace Dime that there were some people who were reluctant to step foot in the great river of life. He had nodded in the direction of Miss Furnace. "These people," he said, "are afraid to love. Loving someone takes a whole lot of courage. Some people just aren't up to the task."

"Ma'am," said Billy Jackson in his most gentle voice, "do you have taper candles?"

Outside the store, Boomer barked several sharp, commanding barks in a row that seemed to say *Give them the candles!*

"Perhaps," sniffed Edna Furnace. "Perhaps I do."

19

The fact that they ended up with forty candles that were different colours and different sizes (and that some of the candles were dusty from having sat for so long on the shelf at the dime store) became irrelevant for a time because when they got back to the house, Pinky and Charisse and Uncle Ted and Ferris's mother were all in the kitchen, and Uncle Ted was holding Pinky upside down by her ankles and shaking her.

It turned out that Pinky – who had been studying the Houdini book and was working to learn how to pick a lock using nothing but a paper clip and her tongue – had ended up swallowing the paper clip by mistake.

She had gone to Charisse's room and said, "I thwallowed it."

"Darling," Charisse said to Ferris later on, "I'm ashamed to say that at first I mistook your sister for the ghost. I was sleeping, and when I woke up and found her standing over me, what I said was, 'My goodness, you are insistent.' A sentiment which, happily, applies to Pinky as well as the ghost."

When Charisse understood what was going on, when she figured out that Pinky wasn't a ghost and that she had swallowed something she shouldn't have swallowed, Charisse ran downstairs, pushing Pinky in front of her and shouting, "Help, help, the child is choking to death!"

Uncle Ted had come running up the stairs from the basement and picked up Pinky and held her upside down and started to shake her.

Which was when Ferris and Billy Jackson and Boomer arrived.

Charisse was sitting at the yellow table. "Hello, darlings," she said when they walked in. "We're having a crisis."

Pinky had her arms crossed over her chest. Even upside down with a paper clip stuck somewhere inside her, she managed to look insouciant.

Insouciant.

Absolutely unconcerned. Indifferent.

"It'th not working," Pinky said as Uncle Ted continued to shake her.

"I don't believe this," said Ferris's mother. "How does someone swallow a paper clip by mistake?"

"Houdini," said Pinky.

The yellow light of late afternoon was throwing itself across the kitchen table, making it brighter, more luminous.

More light.

Charisse put her hand over her heart and looked right at Ferris and smiled and said, "It's so beautiful, darling." And then she toppled over sideways and fell out of the chair and onto the floor.

And all Ferris could think was, *But we got the candles. We just got the candles.*

Everyone went to the medical centre: Charisse and Uncle Ted (in his bathrobe and without shoes) and

Pinky and Billy Jackson and Ferris's mother.

Dr Trench said, "You Wilkeys are keeping us in business."

It turned out that Charisse had fainted from not drinking enough water.

"You have to stay hydrated," said Dr Trench to Charisse. "You have to take care of yourself."

"Certainly," said Charisse in a distant voice. She looked somewhere past Dr Trench as he listened to her heart.

Afterwards, Pinky got an X-ray and they all stood together in the examining room and stared at the paper clip – folded in on itself, floating in her stomach. It looked like a ghost paper clip.

"Wow," said Billy Jackson. He pushed his glasses up with his index finger and leant in closer to the X-ray.

"Waiting is the best course of action," said Dr Trench.

"Waiting for what?" said Pinky.

"What you mean to say is that this too shall pass," said Uncle Ted.

"Exactly," said Dr Trench. And then he said, "Where are your shoes, Ted?"

"I've been studying the human foot recently," said Ted. "It is truly a miracle of design. And also quite challenging to render faithfully." He looked down at his feet and drew his bathrobe tighter.

"I see," said Dr Trench.

Pinky got to take the X-ray of her stomach home. She pinned it to the door of her room, and when Ferris walked by that night after supper, she didn't even think about knocking.

Instead, she went to Charisse's room and spread out the forty candles on the bedspread.

"I'm sorry they don't all match," said Ferris. "Miss Furnace wasn't in a helpful mood."

"She never has been in a helpful mood, darling," said Charisse. "Not in all the years I've known her. This will be wonderful. These candles will work beautifully."

Boomer was sitting at Ferris's feet. He was staring out of the door and panting. He let out a low whimper, and then he stood up and crawled under the bed.

"Charisse?" said Ferris. "Is the ghost here?"

Charisse's eyes were closed.

Ferris stared hard at the doorway. Boomer let out a low moan from under the bed.

A breeze blew through the room.

"I have the candles. We're going to light it tomorrow, I promise," said Ferris to the ghost.

If she was there.

"Of course we are, darling," said Charisse. Without opening her eyes, she reached over and put her hand on top of Ferris's. "Of course we are."

20

The next morning, the exterminator arrived.

The truck said WOOLEY EXTERMINATES, and under the words there was a picture of a rat on his back with his feet up in the air. He had X's where his eyes should be.

The exterminator's name was Glenn. It was embroidered on his shirt in gold cursive letters.

"Are you going to uthe a trap?" said Pinky.

They were in the attic – Pinky and Ferris and their father and Glenn.

"A youth trap?" said Glenn. He wrinkled his forehead.

"Please don't kill them," said Ferris. "Please don't kill the raccoons."

"I'm not going to kill any raccoons," said Glenn.

"I don't see no evidence of raccoons even being up here."

"Dang," said Pinky. She wandered over to a gigantic chest that had the word PHINEAS written on it in peeling gold letters. She sat down on top of the chest and stared at Glenn while he walked around the attic examining things.

"But I've heard them," said Ferris's father. "I've heard raccoons throwing a party, dancing the tango."

"Nope," said Glenn. "I mean, no, sir, you have not. What you got up here is a bee problem."

Right on cue, a bee came buzzing through the molten heat of the attic and flew in a lazy circle around Ferris's head. And then another bee showed up. And a third one.

"They must like something in your hair," said Glenn.

"Ha ha ha," said Pinky from the top of the chest. "Thumone liketh your hair."

And then there were a lot of bees, an overwhelming amount of bees. *A rabble of bees,* thought Ferris, *a swarm.*

Mrs Mielk was very fond of collective nouns. Ferris had memorized a lot of them.

"The trick is not to upset them," Glenn whispered to Ferris. "The trick is – I wonder if you can do this for me, honey – the trick is to pretend like you don't exist."

"OK," Ferris whispered back to him.

"Shhh," said Glenn. "Don't talk. Pretend you aren't here."

Ferris closed her eyes and imagined herself not there. She imagined herself way above the house, looking down into it. She saw Pinky sitting on the Phineas chest, cross-legged and grinning her toothless grin. She saw her father standing next to Glenn looking worried. From up above, she could see that her father had a small bald spot on the top of his head. And then Ferris looked below the attic, below Pinky and her father and Glenn. She saw Boomer standing at the entrance to Charisse's room guarding Charisse while she slept, and on the floor below, Billy Jackson sat at the piano playing "Mysterious Barricades". And in the kitchen, Ferris's mother was at the yellow table putting Green Stamps into a Green Stamps book, and the magnolia tree, standing outside the kitchen window, looked on; and in the basement below her mother, Uncle Ted stood in his bathrobe and stared into the bright white of the almost-empty canvas.

Ferris floated above the house – her house, her world – and everywhere, everywhere there was humming and music and light. She thought, *I am looking down at the great river of life.*

And then the humming stopped.

"Good," whispered Glenn. "Now, that there is a good job. You calmed them bees right down. You can come on back now."

Ferris opened her eyes.

The bees were gone. Glenn the exterminator was smiling at her.

"That was good," he said. "That was a good job, honey. Welcome back."

21

As she went downstairs, Ferris felt light-headed and also relieved. If there weren't raccoons in the attic, then no raccoons would be killed.

In other words, no one would be exterminated.

No one would die.

Boomer came out of Charisse's room wagging his tail at Glenn.

"Hey there, mister," said Glenn.

Boomer wagged his tail harder. Glenn moved his clipboard to his left hand and used his right hand to scratch Boomer behind the ears – first one ear and then the other.

Boomer was so happy with the ear-scratching that he didn't even wag his tail. Whatever he was feeling went beyond tail-wagging. He looked up at Glenn with big-eyed adoration.

The dog was enamoured.

Enamoured was a Mielk vocabulary word.

You wouldn't necessarily think it would apply to dogs and exterminators, but clearly it did.

Downstairs, Billy Jackson was at the kitchen table with Ferris's mother working on affixing Green Stamps into a Green Stamps book. He looked up and smiled at Ferris.

"Hey, Ferris," he said.

"Hey," said Ferris. She sat down next to him. "I thought you were playing the piano."

"I was," said Billy Jackson. "Now I'm helping your ma."

"It turns out we don't have raccoons," said Ferris's father as he walked into the kitchen.

"What do we have?" said her mother.

"Bees," said Glenn. He pulled out a chair and sat down next to Ferris's mother. Boomer sat down too. He leant up against Glenn's legs.

"Now, what we can do here is make up a plan for me to remove that hive for you," said Glenn.

Boomer thumped his tail in approval.

"Bees?" said Ferris's mother. "Bees? How can anyone confuse bees with raccoons?"

"Yet another great mystery that someone will need to unravel at some point," said Ferris's father. "The dogs bark. Et cetera." He opened the refrigerator and stuck his head inside.

Pinky stood in front of Glenn with her hands on her hips. She said, "Have you ever had to ethcape from a trap?"

"Ethcape?" said Glenn. He scratched his head with his pen, and Ferris saw there were words written in red on the white barrel. She tilted her head. *Wooley Exterminates! We Knock 'em Dead!* was what the pen said.

Ferris remembered the rat on the side of Glenn's truck – his feet up in the air, the crosses where his eyes should be – knocked dead.

"Do you know Houdini?" Pinky said to Glenn.

"Who?" said Glenn.

Pinky made a noise of disgust. She turned and left the room.

"OK then," said Glenn. "What I will do is write up this here plan of action for the bee problem, and then you all can decide how you want to proceed." He bent his head over the clipboard and started to write while Boomer sat and stared up at him, dreamy-eyed.

Ferris's father walked over to the table with a stalk of celery. He took a big, loud bite and then he stood and looked over Glenn's shoulder while he wrote.

Ferris stared out of the window at the magnolia tree. She thought about the bees – how they had held still when she pretended she didn't exist, how the whole world had held still. Was that how it felt to be a tree? In the middle of everything but rooted, calm?

Glenn ripped the paper from the clipboard and handed it to Ferris's mother. He said, "Mrs Wilkey, you taught me in ninth grade."

Ferris's mother looked at him. She pursed her lips. "Glenn. Glenn Wooley."

"Yes, ma'am," he said. "It's me."

"You were very good with numbers," said Ferris's mother.

Glenn blushed from his neck all the way up to his forehead. "Yes, ma'am," he said. "I guess so."

Boomer put his head in Glenn's lap. He let out a low woof and Glenn rested his hand on top of Boomer's head for a second, then he pushed back his chair and stood up. "You all can call me when you figure out how you want to proceed."

"Thank you," said Ferris's father. He shook Glenn's hand.

"Bye now, Mrs Wilkey," said Glenn, and he went out the screen door with Boomer trotting along behind him.

Ferris stood up.

"Boomer!" she called, but Boomer ignored her.

By the time Ferris made it outside, Glenn was already in his truck and Boomer was standing in the driveway staring at him longingly.

"Boomer!" Ferris said again.

Boomer turned and looked at her.

"Come here," she said.

Boomer sighed. He trotted over to her.

Glenn Wooley rolled down the window and said, "Ferris, right?"

"Yes, sir," said Ferris.

"You have a way with them bees, Ferris."

"Oh," said Ferris.

She put her hand on top of Boomer's head.

"You got a gift is what I'm saying," said Glenn. "Some people just got a way about them that bees are comfortable with. See you around, Ferris. Bye now, Boomer."

The truck drove away.

"Come on, Boomer," said Ferris.

But Boomer sat down and stared after Glenn Wooley's truck. He had a look of mournful disbelief on his face. He was so mournful that it hurt Ferris's feelings, so she went back into the house without him.

"Ferris?" said Billy Jackson when she walked through the kitchen.

"Did you close that screen door all the way?" said Ferris's mother.

"I'll be right back," said Ferris.

She went through the living room and into the dining room. She stopped to look up at the chandelier and then she climbed the stairs and went into Charisse's room.

Charisse was sitting up in bed with the cards spread out before her, playing solitaire.

"How do you feel?" said Ferris.

"I feel fine, darling. How do you feel?"

"Fine," said Ferris. "The exterminator just left. We don't have raccoons. We have bees."

"Fascinating," said Charisse. "Your father has been hearing the ghost, I would imagine. Not a raccoon."

Ferris thought how upsetting it would be if you were a lovelorn ghost who needed a chandelier lit and someone mistook you for a raccoon.

Charisse put the queen of diamonds down on the king of clubs.

"Also," said Ferris, "there's a big trunk in the attic with 'Phineas' written on it in gold letters."

"A steamer trunk," said Charisse. "It must have

belonged to some travelling Phineas ancestor in days of yore."

"What's in it, do you think?"

"Who knows?" said Charisse. "Who knows how long it has been sitting up there? Decades? Centuries?"

Charisse put a five of clubs down on a six of diamonds.

"Boomer is in love with the exterminator," said Ferris.

"Boomer's in love with everybody, darling," said Charisse. "That's his charm."

"But the exterminator?" said Ferris. She sat down on Charisse's bed. "It's like falling in love with the grim reaper."

"Who told you about the grim reaper?" said Charisse.

"Everyone knows about the grim reaper," said Ferris.

Boomer put his big head around the corner and then came creeping into the room, wagging his tail tentatively. He put his muzzle on Ferris's leg.

Charisse reached over and scratched his ears. "I forgive you, darling," she said.

"Me? Or Boomer?" said Ferris. "And for what?"

"Him," said Charisse. "For loving mightily and widely. It's what we're here for after all."

"But—" said Ferris.

"You are forgiven, Boomer Boy," crooned Charisse.

Boomer closed his eyes in relief.

"Ferris!" Billy Jackson called up the stairs. "Uncle Ted has got the ladder out. Do you want to put the candles in the chandelier now?"

The chandelier! The candles!

Mightily and widely!

"Oh," said Charisse. "The ghost will be so happy, darling. Not only will she no longer be mistaken for a raccoon, but she will see her chandelier lit at last. At last! Go on, now. I feel just fine. I do."

Ferris went down the stairs with Boomer at her heels.

In the dining room, a ladder was set up next to the table and Ted was standing and smiling at her.

He was holding a white envelope in his hands.

He said, "Ferris, honey, before we begin the candle work, I was hoping I could impose upon you to perform an errand of mercy."

22

What Ted wanted was for Ferris to hand-deliver a letter to Shirley at the salon.

As Ted talked about what a favour Ferris would be doing for him, she put her hand up to her head and touched her permed hair.

"Now, don't worry, honey," said Ted. "You don't have to get your hair messed with this time. All you have to do is hand Shirley this little billet-doux."

Billet-doux.

A love letter.

Oh no, thought Ferris.

"You just hand it to her and say, 'I have been told to wait for a reply.'"

"I have been told to wait for a reply," repeated Ferris.

"That's right," said Uncle Ted. He smiled so big that Ferris could see his top back teeth.

"OK, I guess," said Ferris.

"You just run along and do that, and when you get back, you and me and Billy Jackson will get this chandelier all cranked up and ready to shine."

Ferris took the envelope from Ted's outstretched hand. She walked into the kitchen. Her mother and Billy Jackson were back at the table working on the Green Stamps.

"I have to go deliver something," Ferris said to Billy.

"I know it," he said. He pushed his glasses up. He smiled at her.

"Don't let anybody make a fool out of you, Ferris," said her mother.

Ferris touched her hair again. She felt like maybe it was too late to worry about that.

It was busy at Shirley Curl. There were three ladies waiting and reading magazines. A radio next to the reception desk was playing a song about someone's love flying away.

"Fly away, fly away, you flew, my true … love," sang a man mournfully.

It sounded like the kind of song that Boomer would sing to Glenn Wooley. If Boomer could sing.

"Ferris Wilkey!" shouted Shirley. She let out a shriek of disapproval. "What did you do to your hair?"

"What?" said Ferris. "I mean. You gave me a perm."

"You have to *work* with it, honey," said Shirley.

Shirley was able to italicize (emphasize, under-score) words better than anybody Ferris had ever known.

"You can't just perm it and not *style* it," said Shirley. "You can't just walk around hoping that it will work without your *intervention*."

Shirley, scissors in hand, walked away from the lady who was sitting in the beauty chair. She came up to Ferris and studied her more closely. She made a clucking noise that signified both dismay and disapproval.

"Here," said Ferris. She held out the envelope.

Aunt Shirley took several fancy steps back, away from Ferris.

Shirley had very tiny feet, and everything she did on them made it seem like she was dancing.

"Is that from Ted?" asked Shirley. She pointed the scissors at the envelope as she danced further away from Ferris.

"Yes," said Ferris.

Shirley did some more dance steps. She opened and closed the scissors. They made a clicking, vaguely threatening noise.

"That man," said Shirley.

"He told me to wait for a reply," said Ferris.

"The nerve!" said Shirley. "The *nerve* of that man for loving me."

Every good story, thought Ferris. *Every good story is a love story.*

And then she turned to see if Boomer was still outside waiting for her or if he had gone off in search of Glenn the exterminator.

The dog was there, staring in at her through the

glass door. His eyes were worried and his ears were up in the air, as if he was asking her a question.

"He wants a reply!" said Shirley. She stamped one of her tiny feet on the floor and looked around the salon. She snipped her scissors again. "He goes off to paint a history of the world. He leaves *me* to paint a history of the *world*, and he ends up painting a *foot*, and then he wants this child to wait for me while I reply to whatever nonsense he has put in this letter."

Shirley danced forward and grabbed the letter out of Ferris's hand. She used her scissors to cut the envelope open. Someone, at some point, had turned the radio off. It was very quiet inside the Shirley Curl salon.

Shirley tossed the envelope aside; it fluttered slowly to the floor while Shirley stood and silently read the letter.

Outside the salon, the sun was shining. Ferris could feel its warmth through the windows. She could feel the warmth, too, of Boomer's gaze. Ferris held herself still in the same way she had held herself still for the swarming bees.

I am waiting for a reply, thought Ferris. *I am here to wait for a reply.*

And then Shirley was crying – sobbing, really – and Selma Thorpe, who was one of the ladies waiting to get her hair done, was saying, "Shirley, Shirley, whatever is the matter?"

Shirley made a fluttery motion with her hands. The scissors glinted and flashed in the sunlight.

"Aunt Shirley?" said Ferris.

Shirley took a deep, jagged breath. "Yes," said Shirley to Ferris.

"Ma'am?" said Ferris.

"That is my answer. That is my reply. Yes."

"That's what I should tell Uncle Ted?"

"Yes," said Shirley. She stood there crying, holding the letter in one hand and the scissors in the other. She said the word again and then again. "Yes. Yes."

"OK," said Ferris. She turned to go.

Shirley said, "No. Come here. It is *imperative* that I fix your hair before you leave."

"That's OK," said Ferris.

"It won't take but a minute, honey," said Shirley. "Come here."

Which is how Ferris went from a bad perm to a pixie cut.

She sat in the chair and watched as Shirley cut off most of her hair. Hunks of it fell to the ground until there was nothing left on her head but what seemed like a few curls and wisps, the downy feathers of a baby bird.

"Look at you, Emma Phineas Wilkey," Shirley kept saying to Ferris. "Look at those eyes. Who knew you had those eyes?"

When Ferris at last stepped out of the salon, Boomer looked up at her and let out a soft, questioning woof.

"It's me," said Ferris. "I promise."

To prove it, she bent over and let Boomer sniff her head.

23

When Ferris got back home, her mother and Uncle Ted and Billy Jackson were all together in the kitchen peeling potatoes.

"Make sure that screen door closes all the way," said her mother.

"Where's your hair?" said Billy Jackson.

Ferris didn't answer him. Instead, she said to Ted, "Shirley's reply is *yes*."

"Yes?" said Uncle Ted. He turned to her. He was holding a potato in one hand and a paring knife in the other. He had an apron on over his bathrobe. "That's what Shirley said? Yes?"

"Yes," said Ferris.

"Oh," said Ted. "Oh, I believe that I will sit down for just a minute." He moved to the kitchen table and sat down while holding the knife and the potato up above his head.

"Uncle Ted?" said Ferris.

"Yes, honey?"

"Is it not the right answer?"

"It's the right answer," said Ted. He placed the knife on the table and then put the potato next to it. He looked up at Ferris. *"My heart is gladder than all these, because my love is come to me."*

"Save the poetry for later, Ted," said Ferris's mother, who was still peeling potatoes.

"I think I'll make my famous mushroom gravy," said Ted.

"We're planning a big dinner," Billy Jackson said to Ferris. "To eat under the chandelier. There's going to be roast chicken and mashed potatoes."

"Ferris," said Ferris's mother. "Can you explain your hair?"

"No," said Ferris.

"Come here," said Uncle Ted. He held out his arms, and Ferris walked into them. Ted smelled like oil paints. He squeezed her tight. "Thank you, honey," he whispered. "Thank you for sacrificing your hair for me and my beloved."

"You're welcome," said Ferris.

Ted released her. He wiped at his eyes and then he picked up the knife and the potato and started peeling. He said, *My heart is like a singing bird ... because my love is come to me.*"

"Ferris," said her mother. "Maybe you could help with the potatoes, since this was all your idea."

"OK," said Ferris.

But she walked out of the kitchen and went into the dining room. The forty candles were spread out on the table. Ferris looked up at the empty and waiting chandelier and felt a river of words flow through her.

More light and mightily and widely and dust to dust and my heart is like a singing bird and I bequeath myself to grow from the grass I love and every story is a love story and my love is come to me.

She had to see Charisse. She had to tell her, oh, everything ... about the billet-doux and the great river of words and also about how she had calmed the bees.

She had forgotten to tell her about calming the bees.

"Come on, Boomer," said Ferris. He followed her up the stairs and down the hallway to Charisse's room. They both stopped on the threshold.

Pinky was sitting in the window seat.

She was reading aloud to Charisse from the library book about Houdini – *Houdini, Master of Escape!*

"Fascinating, darling," Charisse said to Pinky. "Who wouldn't want to be able to escape from a locked chest?" She then turned to Ferris and raised her eyebrows up very high.

"We're going to put the candles in soon," said Ferris.

"Emmaphineas," said Charisse. "You got your hair cut. You look like a little owl."

Pinky lowered the Houdini book and glared at Ferris. "We're bithy."

Ferris felt as if a small, hard stone was lodged somewhere in her chest. What was Pinky doing on her window seat? What was she doing reading to Charisse?

Boomer looked up at Ferris and then he walked

past her and went into the room and threw himself down on the floor at Pinky's feet. He sighed a huge sigh.

"Good boy," said Pinky. She glared at Ferris. "He'th my dog too."

"OK," said Ferris. "Charisse, I just thought you might want to know about the candles."

"Ferris, darling," said Charisse.

Ferris went down the stairs. She could hear Billy Jackson and her mother and Uncle Ted laughing about something in the kitchen. "Two chickens!" her mother said. And they all laughed some more. It made Ferris feel homesick even though she was already home.

She went out onto the front porch. Her father was sitting in the swing reading the *T* encyclopedia.

"Ah," he said. He lowered the book and smiled at her. "There she is. Ferris, fairest of them all. You got your hair done. Again."

"Aunt Shirley did it," said Ferris.

"I see," said her father. "I must say I like this iteration better."

Iteration was a Mielk vocabulary word. It meant version.

It was good to know so many words and their definitions; but, increasingly, Ferris thought that the world didn't make much sense no matter how many words you knew.

It passeth understanding, thought Ferris. *It passeth all understanding.*

Where were those words from? Had Charisse read them to her? Had she read them to Charisse?

Her father patted the swing. "Come sit beside me, said the spider to the fly."

Ferris sat down. She leant up against her father. "We're going to start putting candles in the chandelier," she said. "And there's going to be a big dinner, and Uncle Ted is happy because Aunt Shirley said yes to something. Pinky's upstairs reading her stupid Houdini book to Charisse. There's a lot going on."

"I've been aware of a great hubbub throughout the house," said her father. "Which is why I thought I would come out here and brush up on my knowledge of the world and its many wonders – as a way to prepare myself for the excitement ahead. Want me to read to you as in days of old?"

When she was very small, just a baby, Ferris's father had read to her from the encyclopedia, and she had listened to him. At least that was the story her father always told. "You were a fussy baby," said her father, "not fussy in the way of crying all the time, but fussy in the way of there was something you were needing to know, something no one was telling you. And one night I thought, *Well, maybe this child wants to hear about the wonders of the world,* so I read to you from the *P–R* encyclopedia. I read you the entry on 'protons'. And you listened with your eyes so wide! Your mother said, 'You're traumatizing the child by reading to her about protons. No baby needs to hear about protons.' But you did. You needed to hear about protons. You stood up in your crib and held on to the bars and listened to me with your eyes all big and bright. Positive-charged protons. You were fascinated. From the beginning you were fascinated, and that is a very good thing to be in this world."

Ferris leant up against her father. He smelt like soap and encyclopedias.

"Yes," she said to him now, "read to me."

There was a lone cricket somewhere on the porch singing a questioning song, and Ferris's father started to read to her about tamarack trees, which were evergreens, and Ferris thought what a good word *evergreen* was. It was a word that promised something. It was a word that had its definition built right into it.

She fell asleep listening to her father read. She dreamt of the steamer trunk in the attic. Bees were buzzing around the trunk and flying in and out of it; and in the dream, when Ferris opened the lid and looked inside, she saw that the chest was filled to overflowing with light. She woke up and her father was still reading, and the cricket was still singing. Billy Jackson came out onto the porch.

"Hello, Billy Jackson," said Ferris's father.

"Hey, Mr Wilkey," said Billy. "Ferris? I been thinking about Mrs Mielk, and I have an idea about what we should do."

Ferris sat up straight.

"What?" she said.

"Mrs Mielk is bereft, right?" said Billy.

Ferris nodded.

"And remember how you said that the word 'bereft' was like a raft that had floated out to sea?"

Ferris nodded again.

"We got to pull in the raft that Mrs Mielk is on," said Billy Jackson.

"I wonder what in the world you children are talking about," said Ferris's father.

"We got to go to Mrs Mielk's and invite her over here," said Billy Jackson. "For the chandelier dinner. I asked your mother if it was OK and she said, 'Why not? Shirley's coming. We might as well have Mrs Mielk too.'"

"Shirley's coming to dinner?" said Ferris.

"Yes," said Billy Jackson. "And then your mother said maybe we should go ahead and invite Glenn the exterminator while we're at it."

"I'm guessing she was joking about that one," said Ferris's father. He closed the encyclopedia and stood up. "Here we go," he said. "The caravan approacheth."

Was *approacheth* a word?

Ferris didn't think so.

But still, she knew what her father meant.

Something momentous was on the horizon, coming towards them.

Or maybe they were moving towards it – walking out to greet it, whatever it was.

24

Mrs Mielk lived two blocks from school. Her house was small and tan-coloured, and the grass around it was mowed and precisely edged. It was an entirely unassuming house. You would never guess that it concealed someone as remarkable as Mrs Mielk.

"You knock," Ferris said to Billy Jackson. "It was your idea."

Billy shook his head. His glasses slipped down his nose and he pushed them back into place. "I can't do it."

Boomer was standing between them, panting nervously. Ferris was just thinking that they should turn around and leave when a grey cat appeared out of nowhere and twined himself through her legs. Boomer, who was terrified of cats, yelped in horror. He leapt off the porch and landed in an azalea bush.

The front door opened and Mrs Mielk appeared before them. Her eyes were red. She was wearing an old sweater and bedroom slippers that looked like dirty pink clouds.

"Billy Jackson," said Mrs Mielk. "Ferris Wilkey."

She said their names like she always said their names.

Emphatically.

Without doubt; clearly.

It was a relief to hear Mrs Mielk sound like herself, even though she didn't look like herself.

"What is your dog doing in my azalea bush?" said Mrs Mielk.

Ferris turned and looked at Boomer. "He's hiding from the cat."

"Hiding," said Mrs Mielk. "I see." She bent down and spoke to the cat. "Come inside now, Samuel Clemens."

The cat went marching into the house with his tail held high.

"The cat is called Samuel Clemens?" said Billy Jackson.

"Correct," said Mrs Mielk. "Samuel Clemens was Mark Twain's given name. Mark Twain was a nom de plume." Mrs Mielk narrowed her red eyes. "Who can define *nom de plume*?"

"A pen name," said Billy Jackson.

"A pseudonym," said Ferris.

Billy Jackson spelt out *nom de plume*, and Mrs Mielk stood up straighter. "That is correct," she said.

"Mrs Mielk," said Billy Jackson when he was done spelling, "we know that you are bereft."

Mrs Mielk nodded. She looked suddenly diminished.

Diminished.

Made less.

Ferris thought about Charisse. Charisse was diminished too. A cold wind blew over Ferris's feet. What happened if someone just kept diminishing? What happened if the diminishment never stopped?

"Do you want to come to a chandelier dinner at my house tonight?" said Ferris.

"A chandelier dinner?" said Mrs Mielk. She blinked. She looked down at her feet in their fuzzy slippers and then she looked back up at Ferris and Billy Jackson. She seemed confused.

"We're going to light an old chandelier using real candles," said Billy Jackson.

"For what purpose?" said Mrs Mielk.

"Because it has never before been lit," said Ferris.

"I see," said Mrs Mielk. "So it would be a christening of the chandelier?"

"I'm not sure," said Ferris.

"Christening," said Mrs Mielk. "A ceremonial first use."

"Yes, ma'am," said Billy Jackson. "It's a christening then."

Ferris looked into Mrs Mielk's grief-stricken eyes. "Please?" said Ferris.

Samuel Clemens came back out onto the porch. He looked in the direction of Boomer, who was still cowering in the azalea bush.

"You children," said Mrs Mielk. She dabbed at her eyes with a crumpled tissue.

"Yes, ma'am," agreed Billy Jackson.

"Thank you," said Mrs Mielk.

"You're welcome," said Ferris.

Mrs Mielk bent down and addressed the cat. "Samuel Clemens, you will leave that dog alone."

The cat let out a single miaow, and then he went back inside. Mrs Mielk stood up.

"I'll see you tonight, children."

"Six o'clock," said Ferris. "My house."

Mrs Mielk nodded. She closed the door softly, and her bereft face and fuzzy pink bedroom slippers disappeared from view.

25

When Ferris and Billy Jackson got back to the house, Allen Buoy was standing on the front porch. He had on a black suit and a red bow tie, and he was holding a bouquet of flowers.

Boomer barked at him.

"Hey, Mr Buoy," said Ferris.

Allen Buoy smiled. He reached up and fiddled with his hearing aid and then he said, "Well, hello. I see that you have had your hair trimmed since we last met."

"Who are the flowers for?" said Ferris.

"Charisse, of course. Charisse, Charisse, forever Charisse." He sighed. "I have been standing here attempting to screw my courage to the sticking place. As Lady Macbeth says. At least I believe it is

Lady Macbeth who says it. In any case, someone in some Shakespeare play talked about courage and screwing it to the sticking place, and the phrase has always resonated with me. Perhaps because when it comes to Charisse, I have been attempting to gather my courage for almost sixty years now."

Mr Buoy pulled a handkerchief out of his jacket pocket and wiped at his forehead.

"You see," he said, "I always knew that she was the one for me, but I never spoke up and she went off and married Fred Wilkey, if you can believe it. I have to say that I couldn't. Believe it, that is. No disrespect intended to your grandfather, but Fred Wilkey – heavens, what a bore." Mr Buoy dabbed at his forehead some more. "I considered writing Charisse a letter, of course…"

Ferris thought of Uncle Ted and his billet-doux to Aunt Shirley and how happy her answer had made him.

My heart is like a singing bird because my love is come to me.

"But," said Allen Buoy, "the time for letter-writing

is past. There is no time left to waste, fritter, dream."

"Do you want me to tell Charisse that you're here?" asked Ferris.

"You could stay for dinner," said Billy Jackson.

But Mr Buoy was not done talking. "I have brought Charisse a bouquet of daisies because I believe them to be an unpretentious flower. They are also the flower of new beginnings. Which is to say that I am done regretting, and that I stand here before you in hope of beginning anew."

Ferris's mother came out onto the porch with a tea towel in her hands.

"Mr Buoy?" she said.

Allen Buoy pivoted on one heel to face Ferris's mother. He held the daisies up above his head. "I have come to proclaim my love," said Mr Buoy. "I have come to claim Charisse."

"Well, for heaven's sake," said Ferris's mother. "What next? You might as well come inside. Along with everyone else."

26

In the dining room Uncle Ted was standing with his hands on his aproned hips, looking up at the chandelier. Ferris looked up too.

"I believe this will be beautiful," Ted said with his head still bent back. "I believe this will be sublime, luminous, numinous, unforgettable. It is time for us to get to work." He lowered his head and pointed at Ferris. "You, Ferris, will be first up the ladder. You will put the first candle in place. And then you will come down the ladder and Billy Jackson will ascend and place the next candle. Up, down; one, then the other. I will hold the ladder. I will supervise."

"Somebody better supervise," said Ferris's mother. "I can tell you that much." She turned and shouted up the stairs. "Charisse! You have a gentleman caller!"

It took a few minutes, but Charisse appeared at the top of the stairs. She descended slowly, holding on to the banister. Mr Buoy was watching her. He held the bouquet of daisies up higher, and then higher still. It was as if the flowers were emitting some kind of light and he wanted to shine their brilliance over the stairway, over Charisse, over the whole house, the wide world.

"Allen Buoy," said Charisse. "Are those flowers for me?"

Pinky came down the stairs behind Charisse. She was holding her Houdini book and scowling at no one in particular. Since when did Pinky follow Charisse everywhere? It was annoying.

Charisse reached the bottom of the stairs and Mr Buoy bowed and handed her the bouquet.

And then he looked at Pinky and said, "I see you are reading about Harry Houdini."

Pinky nodded.

"I will admit to having harboured a lifelong

fascination with Houdini," said Mr Buoy. "It seems I have a talent for harbouring lifelong fascinations." He smiled at Charisse.

Billy Jackson sat down at the piano and started to play "Mysterious Barricades".

The smell of roasting chicken wafted from the kitchen.

"Is a celebration of some sort planned?" Mr Buoy asked the room at large.

"Stay for dinner, Mr Buoy," said Ferris's mother. "Move into the basement and paint a history of the world while you're at it."

"I really don't know much about history," said Mr Buoy.

Charisse stood at the base of the stairs holding the daisies. Their light shone onto her face and she did not look at all diminished. Rather, she seemed enlarged, radiant, immortal.

Every story is a love story.

"Please," said Charisse to Mr Buoy. "Stay for dinner. Stay for the lighting of the chandelier."

27

Pinky demanded, of course, to be a part of things.

"It'th not fair," she said. "I'm alwayth getting left out."

The three of them – Ferris, Billy Jackson and Pinky – took turns going up the ladder and fitting the candles into their holders. Some of the candles didn't fit so Uncle Ted had to shave them with his pocket knife until they were the right size and shape.

When it wasn't his turn to go up the ladder, Billy Jackson went and played the piano. And Pinky, in between her turns, sat beside Mr Buoy. They looked at the Houdini book together.

Boomer stood at the base of the ladder beside Uncle Ted. He watched each of them as they ascended and descended.

The house felt festive. It felt like Christmas. Or maybe like some holiday that they had all forgotten about and were just now remembering.

More light, thought Ferris every time it was her turn to climb up the ladder. *More light.*

At one point she heard Mr Buoy say to Pinky, "Magic, if you ask me, is mostly about believing in yourself so much that you make other people believe in you too."

Charisse was sitting on the other side of Mr Buoy. The two of them were holding hands.

It was almost six o'clock when they finished. The shadows were lengthening and the crickets had started to sing in earnest.

"Now," said Ted. "I must make myself presentable before Shirley arrives. You children set the table."

Ferris and Billy Jackson counted. Her family was five. Billy Jackson was number six. Uncle Ted and Aunt Shirley made eight. Mrs Mielk was nine. Mr Buoy was ten.

Ten people.

Ten place settings under the chandelier.

"Use the good china," said Charisse. "And the Phineas family silver. It has been in the family for a very long time. It could be that she remembers it."

"It could be that *who* remembers it?" said Ferris's mother.

Charisse was saved from having to answer this question by a knock at the front door.

It was Mrs Mielk. She had on a skirt and a blouse but on her feet were the pink bedroom slippers. She must have been so undone by her grief that she forgot to take them off and put on regular shoes.

It made Ferris's heart hurt.

"Come in," she said to Mrs Mielk.

"What about me?" said Shirley. "Should I come in too?"

She was standing behind Mrs Mielk. She was so dressed up that she glittered. As she stepped over the threshold and into the house, Shirley's feet looked tinier than ever, especially next to Mrs Mielk's gigantic slippers of grief.

"Everyone should just come on in," said Ferris's mother.

"Everyone, everyone," said Ferris's father. "The caravan is here."

28

It was dusk and the table was set with the good china and the Phineas family silver, and they all stood together and watched as Ted, clean-shaven and dressed in a suit and tie, went up the ladder with the matches in his hand. He started by lighting the candles in the centre and then he worked his way out and around. It was like watching someone light a birthday cake that had been suspended from the ceiling.

When all the candles were lit, Ted came back down the ladder and folded it up and leant it against the wall.

It was utterly silent in the dining room.

No one spoke, not even Pinky.

Ferris thought that the chandelier was the most

beautiful thing she had ever seen. She thought it was too beautiful for words. Billy Jackson said, "It's like being on the roof of the steakhouse and looking up at the stars."

Ferris nodded. She reached out for Billy Jackson's hand and found it and held it.

"That is truly something to behold," said Ferris's father.

"Magic," said Mr Buoy. He was still holding Charisse's hand. As far as Ferris could tell, he had not let go of it once.

"Well," said Ferris's mother, "we should eat, I suppose."

Billy Jackson said, "I want Pop to see this. He needs to see this." And then he said, louder, "I'm going to go and get my pop."

Before Ferris could stop him or offer to go with him, Billy had run out of the dining room. She heard the screen door in the kitchen wheeze open and close with a half-hearted thud.

"Get another plate, Ferris," said her mother. "Set a place for Big Billy. We'll wait for him."

There were eleven plates under the chandelier then.

Everyone sat down at the table but they kept looking up. You couldn't look away for long. It was too beautiful.

Charisse put her hand on top of Ferris's hand. "Thank you, darling."

"Do you think she's here?" whispered Ferris.

"Not yet," Charisse whispered back. "But I have no doubt that she will appear."

"Should I carve the chickens?" said Ferris's father. "Or should we wait for Big Billy to do that?"

"Wait for Big Billy," said Uncle Ted, who was sitting next to Shirley and who couldn't stop smiling.

Mrs Mielk was looking up at the chandelier. Big tears were rolling down her face and landing on her blouse.

"Mrs Mielk?" said Ferris.

But then Big Billy came into the dining room. Every room that Big Billy entered seemed suddenly smaller and also more filled with life, joy.

"Howdy!" shouted Big Billy to the room at large.

"Look up, Pop," said Billy. "You got to look up."

Big Billy tilted his head and looked at the chandelier. He whistled a long, slow whistle. He said, "You're right, son. Your mama would have loved it. It's just exactly the kind of thing she would have loved."

"Sit down, Big Billy," said Ferris's father. "Let someone feed *you* for a change."

Big Billy sat down next to Mrs Mielk but Billy Jackson stayed standing, looking up at the chandelier and smiling.

"Come sit next to me," Ferris said to Billy. And she thought how it was the same thing she had been saying to him one way or another since the day she first met him.

Big Billy carved the chickens. There were two of them, which was good, because there were more people under the chandelier than anyone had thought there would be.

The dining room windows were open. A breeze came through the room and the candle flames bent in the wind and then came back stronger, more certain.

"It's mushroom gravy," Uncle Ted said to Big

Billy as he passed the gravy boat to him.

"There is a way, I do believe," said Mr Buoy to Pinky. "Yes, indeed, there is a way out of every locked box."

Mrs Mielk was sitting to the left of Billy Jackson. She was holding her fork up to her mouth but there wasn't any food on it.

Another gust of air blew through the room. The candle flames swayed back and forth as if they were dancing, and Ferris wondered if the ghost had arrived.

But it wasn't the ghost. It was moths – a great cloud of them. They appeared all at once, as if they had been conjured. The moths gathered around the lights of the chandelier and flapped their small white wings.

"Look," said Ferris to Billy Jackson.

"I wonder what you call a big old group of moths," said Billy.

Mrs Mielk, her foodless fork still suspended near her mouth, said, "The collective noun for moths is *eclipse*. This is an eclipse of moths."

Eclipse.

An obscuring of light that happens when one celestial body passes in front of another.

Eclipse had been a Mielk vocabulary word.

Charisse suddenly leant in very close to Ferris, and Ferris smelt Florida water and baby powder. "Turn around and look, darling," whispered Charisse. "Look at the stairs."

Ferris turned slowly and looked at the stairs. There was nothing there.

"It's her," breathed Charisse. "And she is holding someone. She is being held."

"Who's holding her?" said Ferris. She couldn't see anything except for the wooden banister gleaming in the light of the candles.

"It's her husband, darling," said Charisse. "At least I assume it's her husband. He's wearing a uniform. Oh, it's so wonderful. He has found his way to her at last."

Another great gust of air went through the room. The white-winged moths disappeared en masse (in a group, all together), and from somewhere there came an otherworldly sound of grief and despair.

29

What in the world is Boomer howling about?" said Ferris's mother.

The wind blew through the room with greater force. The candle flames swayed and flickered and then they all went out. It was as if some giant had bent over the house and made a wish – blowing out the candles with one great breath.

The dining room was suddenly dark.

The howl of despair sounded again – louder this time, and even more desperate.

"Is it the ghost?" Billy Jackson said to Ferris.

"Ted?" said Shirley.

"I'm right here, darling," said Ted.

Ferris's father got up and turned on the lamp on the sideboard.

"Well, it was exciting while it lasted," said Ferris's mother.

Ferris looked around the table. Pinky's seat was empty.

"Pinky?" said Ferris. She looked under the table and saw Mrs Mielk's tragic bedroom slippers and everyone else's feet, but no Pinky.

And no Boomer.

Ferris stood up. "Boomer is in trouble and Pinky is missing."

"What in the world is your sister doing now?" said Ferris's mother. "Go find her, Ferris."

A strangled *yelp* emanated from the kitchen.

Ferris forgot about Pinky.

She ran to the kitchen and found Boomer cowering in a corner staring at a raccoon, who was perched on top of the yellow table.

The raccoon was holding the Green Stamps sponge in one paw. Green Stamps were scattered everywhere and the raccoon was hissing at Boomer and showing him his teeth, and also waving the sponge back and forth in a threatening way.

Boomer whimpered.

From the dining room came the clatter of forks on plates, laughter, talk.

"OK, OK," said Ferris to Boomer and the raccoon.

The raccoon turned and hissed at her. He waved the sponge around, and Ferris thought how it would have been good if Glenn the exterminator *had* been invited to dinner.

The raccoon turned back to Boomer. He snarled some more.

Boomer trembled.

The three of them – Ferris and Boomer and the raccoon – were frozen in a tableau of horror.

Tableau.

A group of motionless figures representing a scene from a story or history.

But which was this, Ferris wondered. History or a story?

And where was everybody else? And why didn't someone come and look for her?

From where Ferris was standing, she could see the magnolia tree outside the kitchen window; its trunk was visible even in the darkness. The magnolia tree would be the only witness to what happened next – whatever it was.

Ferris heard the scraping sound of chairs being pushed back from the table, and then came music – Billy Jackson playing "Mysterious Barricades".

"Well, I brought a fridge cake for dessert," said Shirley from the dining room. "Because I know that a fridge cake is Ted's absolute *favourite* and always has been."

Boomer looked at Ferris. His eyes were huge. The fur on his ears was trembling.

"Now Ferris is missing too," said Ferris's mother.

"I love you, Boomer," said Ferris. Because it felt like something important was happening, and also because it seemed possible that she and Boomer would die together at the hands – paws; no, actually, *teeth* – of the raccoon.

Ferris thought of the dead rat on the side of Glenn Wooley's truck, his crossed-out eyes, his feet in the air. And then she remembered the bees and how she had calmed them by pretending not to exist.

Would that work with a raccoon?

It was worth a try.

And so Ferris pretended. She closed her eyes and went somewhere out of her body and above the house.

She could see the dining room. She could see Mr Buoy and Charisse holding hands (still). She could see Uncle Ted and Aunt Shirley laughing, and Big Billy and her father talking together – Big Billy nodding and her father smiling. She could see her mother picking up the plates from the table one by one.

She could see Billy Jackson in the living room playing the piano, and Mrs Mielk standing over him, tapping her pink bedroom slippers in time to Billy's playing and crying, crying, crying.

Ferris could see the candles in the chandelier, the melted wax on them. She could see a single white moth circling the candles – looking for the light, wondering where it all had gone.

Ferris went higher – beyond the unlit chandelier and the lonesome moth, up the stairs and past the bedrooms and into the attic, where the bees were, where the Phineas chest sat on the bare boards.

And Ferris remembered the dream she'd had that afternoon – how the bees had gone in and out of the trunk, how the inside of it had been filled with light.

Look in the trunk, she said to herself. *Open the trunk, Ferris, and look inside.*

And she did.

She opened the trunk. And what she saw inside was Pinky.

Pinky was trapped.

Pinky was in the trunk with the lid closed, and she could not escape.

"Oh," said Ferris. "Pinky."

And with those words she came back to earth, to the kitchen, to the raccoon, to Boomer, to the yellow table and the Green Stamps and the magnolia tree.

"Pinky is in the trunk!" she shouted. "Help, help! A raccoon is in the kitchen and Pinky is in the trunk!"

"Ferris?" said Billy Jackson. He was right behind her. He put his hands on her shoulders.

And then Ferris's father was there too. "Holy Moses," he said. "I knew it. I knew we had raccoons."

Big Billy came out into the kitchen. He said, "How about we open the screen door and let this big fella leave? I bet you he would be glad to just walk on out of here."

"That raccoon has my sponge," said Ferris's mother.

Big Billy walked over to the door. He opened it and went outside and held the door open wide. "Come on now, Mr Raccoon," he called.

The raccoon looked right at Ferris. He raised his upper lip and showed her his teeth. And then he dropped the sponge and leapt off the table and waddled across the kitchen floor. There was a Green Stamp stuck to his tail and he was in no hurry at all. He took the time to stop in front of Boomer and snarl at him up close.

Boomer keeled over on his side and showed the raccoon his pink, trembling stomach; the raccoon, satisfied, walked past Boomer and out the open door and into the night.

"Just keep moving!" shouted Ferris's mother after the raccoon. "And Big Billy, will you please make sure that screen door closes all the way?"

"Pinky," said Ferris. "We have to get Pinky. Pinky is trapped."

"For heaven's sake," said her mother, who was bent over picking Green Stamps up from the floor. "Trapped where?"

"She's upstairs," said Ferris. "In the attic. Inside the steamer trunk."

Ferris's mother stood up and looked at Ferris. Her face was drained of all colour. "She's inside the trunk?"

"What did she say?" said Mr Buoy. He was standing with Charisse at the entrance to the kitchen. "What did the child just say?"

"Pinky is trapped in the trunk in the attic!" shouted Ferris.

"Lord help us," said Mr Buoy. He dropped Charisse's hand. He said to Ferris, "Show me."

30

Mr Buoy and Mrs Mielk were the ones who got to the attic first. They were the ones who opened the steamer trunk.

Pinky was inside with her hands crossed on her stomach and her mouth hanging open. She looked like Sleeping Beauty, minus a few teeth. She wasn't moving.

"NO!!!" shouted Ferris's mother. "Absolutely not!"

"I am a trained EMT!" Mrs Mielk shouted back. "Help me lift her. I am a trained EMT!"

Mr Buoy and Mrs Mielk reached into the trunk together and lifted Pinky out.

She looked so small.

How could Pinky be that small?

They placed her gently on the floor and Mrs

Mielk tilted Pinky's head back and breathed into her mouth.

One of Mrs Mielk's pink slippers had fallen off. It was on the floor by Pinky's head, and Ferris thought it was the saddest thing she had ever seen.

Mrs Mielk sat back on her heels. She gently shook Pinky. "Come on, sweetheart," she said.

Pinky suddenly sat up straight and shouted, "Out of my way, foolth!" And then she fell back onto the floor.

"How's that?" said Mr Buoy. "What did she say?"

"She said, 'Out of my way, fools,'" said Ferris.

"She's fainted again," said Mrs Mielk.

Ferris's mother was on her knees beside Pinky. "Pinky!" she shouted. "Snap out of it!"

"Come on now, Pinky," said Ferris's father. He was crying.

Ferris's knees felt wobbly.

Pinky.

She sat down on the floor next to Pinky's head. She put her hand on her sister's forehead, and Pinky's eyes fluttered open.

"Thtop it," said Pinky.

"Pinky," said Ferris.

"What?" said Pinky.

Which was when Ferris started to cry too.

You have waded deeper into the great river of life.

Somewhere in the attic a bee was buzzing.

"You're my sister," said Ferris.

"Duh," said Pinky. She sat up.

"I love you," said Ferris to Pinky.

"Let's get this child downstairs where's it cooler," said Mr Buoy.

"Also," said Mrs Mielk, "she needs to be hydrated."

"I love you," Ferris said to Pinky again.

"I heard you the firth time," said Pinky.

31

Ferris couldn't sleep. She walked down the hall to Charisse's room and stood on the threshold and waited until she could see Charisse's chest rising and falling. And then she went to Pinky's room and opened the door and stepped inside. Pinky was asleep on her back with her arms and legs spread wide. She was snoring a little.

Ferris went down the stairs and into the dining room. She stood and looked up at the chandelier. The candles were still in it; its arms were still outstretched.

"How did you know where your sister was?" Mrs Mielk had asked when everyone was leaving that night. "How did you know where to look?"

Ferris thought about the dream – the trunk and

the bees and the light. She thought about being above the house and looking down into it. How could she explain all of that to Mrs Mielk? What was the word that described how she knew?

Intuition?

Hunch?

Divination?

"I don't know," she said to Mrs Miclk.

"In any case," said Mrs Mielk, "it's good that you figured it out. Your sister was in very grave danger."

It wasn't until Mrs Mielk left, until everyone had left, that Ferris realized what the word was that described how she knew where Pinky was.

Love.

It was a word that Mrs Mielk had not needed to teach her.

It was a word that Ferris had known her whole life.

When Ferris walked out into the kitchen she found her mother sitting at the yellow table playing solitaire.

"I couldn't sleep," said Ferris.

"Yep," said her mother. "Neither could I."

"Mrs Mielk said that Pinky was in very grave danger," said Ferris.

Her mother looked at her and nodded once – a solemn nod, a nod from one grown-up to another.

Ferris's knees felt weak. She sat down at the table.

"I'll make you some hot milk," said her mother. "With cinnamon and honey. Does that sound good?"

"Yes," said Ferris.

Her mother got up and went to the refrigerator, and Ferris sat and looked out of the window at the trunk of the magnolia tree – dark and patient, straight and true.

Boomer slunk into the kitchen, looking around and wagging his tail just the tiniest bit.

"It's OK," Ferris told him. "The raccoon is gone."

Boomer gave her a tragic look, and then he lay down at her feet with a huge sigh.

Ferris had stood on the porch that night and watched everybody leave – Mrs Mielk and Mr Buoy, Billy Jackson and Big Billy Jackson, Uncle Ted and Aunt Shirley.

Uncle Ted had walked down the front path with his arm around Shirley's shoulders; but then he had stopped and turned around and come back up the steps and bent over and kissed Ferris on the cheek.

"Thank you, honey," he said.

"For what?"

"For all of it. I hope the ghost is as happy as I am."

"Did you see the ghost?"

"No," said Ted. "Did you?"

Ferris shook her head. "Charisse saw her, though. Charisse said she was there. Do you believe in ghosts, Uncle Ted?"

Ted rubbed his cheeks. He looked up at the sky and then back down at Ferris. "There was a writer named Bede who lived a long time ago."

"Ted!" shouted Shirley.

Uncle Ted turned and said, "In a minute, darling." And then he turned back to Ferris and said, "Bede wrote that we are like sparrows who fly through the great feasting hall of a castle."

"I don't understand," said Ferris.

"No one knows what comes before or after the

feasting hall," said Ted. "We just know that we fly into it and then, later, we have to fly on back out – into the unknown."

"OK," said Ferris. She still didn't understand.

"But tonight, honey – tonight we were sparrows in the feasting hall. We were at a banquet, and we knew it. What I'm saying is that it was a good party."

Ted had put his hand on her head for just a minute, blessing her again, before he went back down the steps and into the darkness.

Ferris's mother came back to the table with two cups. "It was a big night," she said.

Ferris nodded.

"And it was beautiful, too," said her mother. "It was beautiful – sitting at the table together and looking up at that chandelier."

Boomer wagged his tail slowly back and forth as if he was agreeing with everything Ferris's mother said.

"When you were born…" said her mother. She picked up the cards and shuffled them.

Ferris sat up straighter. She held her breath. Her

mother never talked about when Ferris was born. It was Charisse and Ferris's story, and Charisse was the one who told it.

Boomer put his head on top of Ferris's foot.

"When I was born," said Ferris to her mother.

Her mother sighed. "The thing about your father's side of the family," she said, "the thing about the Wilkeys, is that they never pass up a ride of any sort. I mean this literally and metaphorically. They never pass up excitement. That day at the fair, your father said, 'Look, the Ferris wheel! Let's go! A Ferris wheel is the most benign ride there is. Nothing can go wrong.' And Charisse said, 'Let's go! It will be divine!' And so we went. Even though I felt like it was wrong to be so far away from the ground, the earth, when I knew that you could be arriving at any minute. But I let myself get talked into it."

Her mother put the cards down. She looked out of the window.

Boomer was asleep and snoring in a wheezy kind of way. His feet were moving. He was chasing something. Or running away from something. The raccoon, most likely.

"And then we were up there," said her mother. "We were at the top of the Ferris wheel, at the very top, and I looked down and it was all so beautiful, the world. You forget, sometimes, how beautiful it is. That's what the chandelier made me think of tonight: being at the top of the Ferris wheel. Everything was so bright and beautiful and *possible*, you know?"

"Yes," said Ferris. She was afraid to say more because she didn't want her mother to stop talking.

"Anyway, that was what I was thinking when my waters broke. Your father shouted, 'Holy smokes, we're having a baby up here! We're having a baby right now! Bring us down!' And we came down. And I had you right there on the fairground underneath the Ferris wheel. Charisse knew just what to do. She didn't panic at all. And suddenly, you were here."

"And suddenly, I was here," repeated Ferris.

A breeze came in through the open window and brought with it the smell of grass and stars. At Ferris's feet, Boomer dreamed and dreamed.

The floorboards creaked. Ferris's father came into the kitchen in his pyjamas. His hair was standing up on top of his head. "What are you two doing?"

"We couldn't sleep," said Ferris.

"Should I read to you?" said her father. Without waiting for an answer, he shuffled out of the kitchen and returned holding the *N–O* volume of the encyclopedia. Pinky was walking behind him.

"Look who I found," said her father.

Pinky.

"Pinky," said Ferris. And she couldn't believe how glad she was to see her.

"Yeth," said Pinky. "It'th me." She lay down on the floor and wrapped her arms around Boomer. She put her head on his flank. "Read," she commanded.

Ferris's father read the entry on Napoleon, a short man who once had been an emperor. Pinky fell asleep with her face buried in Boomer's fur, and Ferris fell asleep with her head on the kitchen table. She dreamt of a Ferris wheel that had words painted on the base of it. Great gold letters – gilded letters – that spelled out *Emma Phineas.*

Mrs Mielk was standing by the Ferris wheel, pointing at the words.

"Look at this," she said. "Look at these beautiful words."

The next thing Ferris remembered was her parents ushering her and Pinky up the stairs.

"There you go," said her father. "Up, up, up."

From above them came the sound of snoring. Charisse insisted that she didn't snore, that she was too much of a lady to snore. But she was snoring.

Boomer was ahead of them on the stairs, and he kept turning and looking back to make sure that they were there, following him.

"Here we are," Ferris said to him again and again. "We're all here."

32

The ghost did not return, but Allen Buoy came to the Wilkey house every day. He went up to Charisse's room and played cards with her. He read to her from Whitman and the Bible, and Boomer crossed the threshold into Charisse's room without hesitation or fear.

Autumn came.

Pinky entered first grade.

Ferris and Billy Jackson went into fifth grade.

Sometimes Ferris saw Mrs Mielk in the hallway at school. Mrs Mielk always nodded at Ferris, and Ferris nodded back. It was as if they had some great unspoken thing between them – a grave danger they had averted together.

"Do you think the ghost will ever come back?"

Ferris asked Charisse one afternoon after Mr Buoy had left.

"Why in the world would she?" said Charisse. "She has nothing to keep her here. The chandelier was lit at last. Her beloved found his way home to her."

Later that year, in the winter, when Charisse was in hospital, Ferris sat beside her and held her hand and asked her not to leave.

"Darling," said Charisse.

Ferris put her head down on the hospital bed. She didn't want Charisse to see her cry. "But if you leave," said Ferris, "maybe you could come back?"

"Come back!" said Charisse. "There's no need for me to come back. I have no regrets. I've left nothing undone. It's been wondrous, darling. Wondrous."

"Do you remember?" said Ferris.

"Remember what, darling?"

"Remember how you caught me when I was born?"

"How could I ever forget? Who could ever forget such a thing?"

At the funeral Billy Jackson played "Mysterious Barricades". Later that night he told Ferris he didn't think he would ever play the song again. "It was like the music was some kind of door to somewhere, and playing it over and over again pushed open the door just enough to get to the other side of something. I don't need to play it any more. Does that make sense?"

"No," said Ferris, "but I believe you."

They were on the roof of the steakhouse and it was cold. Still, they lay on their backs and looked up at the stars. Ferris couldn't stop crying.

"We should light the chandelier again," said Billy Jackson.

"OK," said Ferris.

"Every year at the same time, we'll light it and have dinner underneath it. All right?"

Down below, Boomer let out a low woof. And then came the *whap-whap-whap* of his tail hitting the side of the building. Pinky's head appeared at the top of the ladder. Her blonde hair shone in the light of the steakhouse sign. Her face was streaked with tears.

"Pinky," said Ferris.

"Move over," said Pinky.

Ferris moved over, and Pinky lay down between Ferris and Billy Jackson. "I loved her too," said Pinky. "She was mine too."

The three of them cried together on the roof of Big Billy's Steakhouse. Inside the restaurant, Bob Munson was playing the piano and Billy Jackson's mother was smiling at him as he played. Ferris couldn't hear it or see it, but she knew it was happening.

Boomer whined. He barked once.

"It's OK," Ferris called down to him. "We're OK."

After Charisse died, Uncle Ted started work on his painting again.

He would come to the house late in the afternoon and go down into the basement, and sometimes Ferris went and sat with him.

"Is it still going to be a history of the world?" she asked Ted.

"Patience, honey, patience."

Slowly, afternoon by afternoon, a world appeared beneath Ted's brush: there was a table and there were people sitting at the table and their faces were upturned, catching the light from above, catching the light from the candles in the chandelier. Moths flitted around the flames.

"It's us," said Ferris.

"It is," said Ted.

"It's us in the feasting hall," said Ferris.

"That's right," said Ted.

When the painting was done you could see that, way up in the far corner of the canvas, there was a small brown-feathered bird – a sparrow.

The sparrow was flying through the room. Her wings were outstretched, and she was so small and unassuming that most people didn't even notice her.

But Ferris knew she was there.

Ferris knew there was a sparrow in the feasting hall.

Coda

It was spring when Uncle Ted and Aunt Shirley's baby arrived.

Ferris and Pinky and Billy Jackson went to the hospital to see her.

The three of them leant together over the crib.

"Move," said Pinky to Ferris. "You're taking up too much space. Let me see her."

Ferris moved to the side. She watched Pinky make faces at the baby – sticking her thumbs in her ears and waggling her fingers, sticking out her tongue.

"Stop it," said Ferris. "You'll scare her."

"No, I won't," said Pinky. "She likes it. I can tell."

Billy Jackson stood staring down at the baby and smiling. He was humming.

Ferris leant way over into the crib. She put her face close to the baby's face.

"Hey, darling," Ferris whispered.

The baby smiled at her like she knew her, recognized her.

"Babies don't smile when they're that young," said Ferris's mother. "It was probably gas."

But Ferris knew. It was a smile.

The baby's name was Charisse Rose Wilkey.

"Welcome," Ferris whispered to the baby. "Welcome, darling. Here we are."

KATE DiCAMILLO, one of America's most beloved storytellers, is the author of *The Tale of Despereaux* and *Flora & Ulysses: The Illuminated Adventures*, both of which have been awarded the prestigious Newbery Medal; *Because of Winn-Dixie*, which received a Newbery Honor; *The Miraculous Journey of Edward Tulane*, which won a *Boston Globe–Horn Book* Award; and the bestselling Mercy Watson series. Born in Philadelphia, she grew up in Florida and now lives in Minneapolis, USA.